W.

MW01114641

""Naughty or Nice is a great anthology. The stories are fun, the Christmas season is always well-represented, and each of these stories has a little something that really catches your interest. One great anthology, three great reads." - *Ann Leveille for Sensual Romance*

"Three erotic stories to spice up Christmas!" - *Sime~Gen, Inc.*

"Make room on your must-read-Christmas list for Naughty or Nice. It's not to be missed." - *Ayden Delacroix, In the Library*

Discover for yourself why readers can't get enough of the multiple-award-winning publisher Ellora's Cave. Whether you prefer e-books or paperbacks, be sure to visit EC on the web at www.ellorascave.com for an erotic reading experience that will leave you breathless.

www.ellorascave.com

Ellora's Cave Publishing, Inc.
PO Box 787
Hudson, OH 44236-0787

ISBN # 1843605740

Edited by Cris Brashear.
Cover art by Darrell King.

Warning: The following material contains strong sexual content meant for mature readers. *NAUGHTY OR NICE* has been rated R and NC17 erotic, by a minimum of three independent reviewers. We strongly suggest storing this book in a place where young readers not meant to view it are unlikely to happen upon it. That said, enjoy…

NAUGHTY OR NICE

Jingle's Belle
Lani Aames
-7-

The Twelve Nights of Christmas
Treva Harte
-79-

Santa Claws
Maryjanice Davidson
-139-

JINGLE'S BELLE

Written by

LANI AAMES

December 18

Christmastown, The North Pole

Present Day

All the elves in Workshop #7 snickered when Jingle's name was called over the loudspeaker and he was directed to report to the Main Office immediately. Jingle ignored the other elves at their workbenches as he strode past them, shrugged into his heavy coat, and pulled on his boots. He closed the door firmly behind him without a backward glance.

The night air was cold and crisp this day...but the air was always cold and crisp at The North Pole and this time of year it was always night. Jingle enjoyed watching *Baywatch* every day after work, but he couldn't really imagine what it would be like to live near a body of water warm enough to swim in, a stretch of sand to wiggle bare toes in, or sunlight strong enough to turn pale skin a golden brown. Jingle had lived his entire life in Christmastown and had never ventured south of the Arctic Circle.

Trudging across the ice with the colorful flares of the Aurora Borealis lighting his way, Jingle wished he had time to stop by the stables. For years, he'd been trying to get a job as reindeer trainer, but he always managed to mess up when the time came for promotions. He often stopped by after work to watch the reindeer play instead of socializing at the Icicle Inn like the others. He hardly ever visited the pub. No one wanted him around. Not even Tinsel, the prettiest elfess in the world.

Jingle reached the Main Office much too soon. What could Santa want with him? What had he done wrong now? Nothing...that he could remember.

Inside, he removed his coat and boots. He straightened his dark green uniform as best he could, but the shirt and trousers always hung loose on his small frame. He couldn't help it if he was the shortest and smallest elf of all, and not even size minus-half-elven fit him quite right. He hitched up his trousers and tightened the belt fastened over his shirt, but it didn't help the drooping shoulder seams or sagging crotch.

Nervously, he ran a hand through his unruly hair, trying to smooth the long black curls that always hung in disarray, wishing for the gazillionth time in his life that it was a light shade like all the other elves. Why did he have to have hair the color of black ice and tan skin that looked as if he'd stepped out of *Baywatch* instead of the normal pale elven complexion? He hoped Santa wouldn't be disappointed in him — again. He knocked on The Door and entered when a muffled voice told him to.

The large room was lined with shelves stuffed with countless letters and reams of lists. Tinsel was setting a box in the middle of the cluttered desk. She was dressed neatly in her forest green uniform, the points of her shirt hanging perfectly off her hips and across her thighs. Jingle's breath caught in his chest when she turned to see who had entered. He smiled at her.

Golden hair was tucked behind her ears, crystal stud earrings winking from just inside the peaks. How many nights had he lain awake imagining Tinsel moaning in ecstasy as he ran his fingers over those delectable points?

Too many, he thought when she stared at him blankly then turned back toward the desk with a cheerful smile.

"Will that be all, sir? I need to get back to Records and straighten up."

From behind a stack of ledgers, a hand waved at her in dismissal.

Jingle smiled again as she came toward him on her way out. "Hi, Tinsel. Nice weather we're having," he said inanely, wishing he had a way with words, other than sounding stupid.

Tinsel flounced past him without a look or word, and Jingle's heart fell into the pit of his stomach. Why had he ever expected any different from her? Who could blame her or any elfess? He wasn't much taller than she, and he looked awful in his ill-fitting uniform. Why should she notice him when everyone knew she was seeing Zap, Senior Reindeer Trainer. Zap stood over a head taller than Jingle and wore a size extra-double-elven uniform as if the material had been woven around his body.

"Alexander?" a voice called gruffly from behind the ledgers.

Jingle winced and his face flushed with embarrassment at Santa's use of his given name. He was glad Tinsel had already left the room. The name he had been given at birth was another reason for ridicule from the others. Alexander was a human name, not elven. It had taken him years to make everyone forget the name Alexander and use the name he'd chosen for himself — Jingle, a proper elven name. Everyone except Santa, of course. Santa never forgot anything.

"Yes, sir," Jingle finally said and stepped closer to the desk. "You wanted to see me?"

Santa set aside a list he had finished checking twice—Jingle noticed the bold double checkmarks—and stood. The jolly old elf towered over Jingle. He drew up, stiffened his back and straightened his shoulders, trying not to appear too small, but Santa was still the tallest elf he knew. Santa was even taller than Zap!

"Good to see you, lad," Santa said as he walked around the desk at a sprightly gait. "How are things going in Number Seven?"

"Right on schedule, as planned," Jingle said. Actually, they were ahead of schedule, but anything could happen. He didn't want to boast and then have them lose time, barely making production. It had happened before.

"Number Seven has always been my favorite. Did you know it's the original workshop?"

"Yes, sir. Those of us who work in Number Seven are proud to continue the tradition."

Santa shook his head wearing a sad frown. "I know there isn't much call for wooden toys these days. All the children want toys made out of plastic and electronics. Oh, well, times change and we have to change with them. I've always regretted not naming it Number One, but the Missus talked me into numbering them by location, and that one was built before we drew up the plans for Christmastown. She's the practical one."

"How is Mrs. Claus?"

"Busy as always with her baking."

"Please give her my regards," Jingle added affectionately.

Everyone loved Mrs. Claus and she loved every one of them. She called him Alexander, too, but he didn't mind her using the human name. He had spent many afternoons

12

at her kitchen table, eating tons of cookies and fruitcake and strudel, and drinking tall glasses of her Special Reindeer Milk. At the time, he thought eating enough would make him as big and tall as the other elves, but nothing had helped.

"I'll tell her, lad." Santa lifted the box Tinsel had set on the desk. "Come along, Alexander. I'm sure you're curious why I called for you."

Jingle followed him to the back of the room and through a door, which led to a smaller, cozier room—Santa's study. Jingle had never been in this room and didn't know anyone who had. He held his breath as he stepped over the threshold, and Santa closed the door behind them.

A fire crackled in the fireplace, a rarity in Christmastown. None of the elves knew exactly how their homes and shops were heated, but there were no fireplaces in any of them. Lumber was brought in, of course, but it was for the making of wooden toys in #7. Jingle had never seen actual logs like those burning in the fireplace, except on the television of course.

Two overstuffed chairs set in front of the fireplace, a table between them holding a lamp and a large snowglobe. To one side was an antique cabinet, and the rest of the walls were covered in shelves filled with books.

"This is my private study, where I get away from time to time. No one is allowed in here, not even the cleaning elves. And Mrs. Claus comes only at my invitation. This close to Christmas, I usually don't have time to slip in here. But I've got a little problem and I think you can help me out. Sit down, Alexander, and make yourself comfortable."

Jingle sat in the chair that looked the least worn, deciding the other would be Santa's favorite. He settled in, feeling dwarfed as the plump upholstery enveloped him. Only the toes of his shoes touched the floor. Yes, even the furniture was made to accommodate extra-double-elven sized elves.

Santa handed him a small glass of sherry and sat in the other chair.

"I don't know how I can help," Jingle said after taking a sip of the dry wine. "But I'll do anything you ask."

"You're a good lad, Alexander, to agree to help before you know what the problem is. If you'd rather not, just say the word." Santa moved the snowglobe closer to Jingle. "Look in there and tell me what you see."

Jingle set the sherry glass aside. The glass ball, balanced on an ornate gold base, was large enough that he would have trouble holding it in both hands. A tiny blizzard spun dizzily within. Jingle looked but he saw nothing except the snow.

"Sorry, lad, I forgot," Santa said and passed his hand over the globe.

The swirling snow cleared in the center and a form took shape. As it sharpened, Jingle saw it was a human woman. She was beautiful, he decided, for a human. Her eyes were large, almost elven, except they were a dark color. Her long dark brown hair was pulled back in a ponytail and one round ear was visible.

All humans had round ears, and he'd seen many of them on the television, but he was still intrigued by the way the top curved instead of coming to a point like elven ears. Did fondling their ears arouse humans the same way it did elves? Ears were hardly ever mentioned or touched on the television. He'd always thought maybe it was too intimate a gesture to show, but he wasn't sure. He'd seen most intimate gestures enacted on the television — gestures he'd imagined trying with Tinsel if she had ever noticed him.

This human woman was as beautiful as Tinsel, he surprised himself by thinking.

"Her name is Belinda Cooper," Santa said as he shuffled papers in the box, looked at one, discarded it, and picked up another. "She was a wonderful child, never asking for outrageous presents like most children. She began to unbelieve when she was eight years old."

Unbelieve. The word brought incredible sadness to them all. Every time a child started to unbelieve, a little of the magic of Christmas was lost.

"I haven't heard from her in a long time, of course," Santa continued. "Belinda grew up and started living her life. She's twenty-nine now."

Jingle frowned. Humans lived such short lives compared to elves. At the equivalent of twenty-nine human years, he had still been considered an immature elfling. Even now, he was quite young compared to most of the other elves in Christmastown.

"Belinda is all alone. Her father died when she was a child, and her mother five years ago, both near Christmas, which brings sad memories during the holiday season. She has no husband, no children, no one to call her own. Belinda's Christmas spirit is nearly broken."

Jingle nodded. He understood that humans considered death as a devastating loss while elves regarded it as a cause for celebration. But elves did not die the same way as humans. Their *fading* was a return to the

Elfland, the origin of their existence. Jingle missed his mother Twilight, but he wasn't sad. He knew she had returned to the Elfland and he was happy for her. All elves anticipated their eventual return to the Elfland.

His father? It was unheard of among elves not to know one's parents, yet he'd never known his father. It was the only thing Twilight ever denied him — information about his father. When asked why she'd given him a human name, she explained she liked the sound of it, but would say no more. Jingle suspected there was much more to it than that, but he had never persisted.

"I'm not supposed to have favorites among the children, you know," Santa said, breaking into Jingle's thoughts. "But Belinda was a special child. Don't tell the Missus, but she always left the best cookies I've ever eaten."

Jingle smiled at Santa's confession, but he was puzzled. He wasn't sure what Santa thought he could do. As if reading his mind, Santa answered his question.

"I want you to help Belinda regain her Christmas spirit. She's very sad and lonely and needs a special friend right now. Christmas is only a week away, and she hasn't even begun to decorate. Now, it will be obvious from the moment you arrive, that you're not human. But she won't — or won't *want* to believe you're elven. You'll have to convince her that you're one of my elves and there is much to be thankful for, that her blessings outweigh the sadness. It will be a difficult task."

Jingle stared at the still picture of the human called Belinda Cooper. Moving among humans would not be easy, but his life with the elves had never been easy either. Most of all, Santa asked this of him and he would never say no to Santa.

"I'll do it," Jingle said in a quick rush of breath before he could change his mind.

"Good! I'm sure you'll do an excellent job, Alexander," Santa said proudly. "It's the middle of the night there now. We'll leave as soon as the team is hitched up."

Jingle watched as the picture of Belinda Cooper slowly faded, to be replaced by the snowstorm. He wasn't sure how to go about helping her regain her Christmas spirit, but with his pointed ears and small stature, he would have no trouble convincing her he was an elf.

December 19

Glenville, Tennessee

Present Day

Belinda Cooper lay awake in her darkened bedroom and tried to sleep, but she was restless. She raised up on one elbow to punch her pillow into a more comfortable shape, then she flopped down on her stomach. The red numerals on the digital clock screamed 1 a.m. at her. Bel wanted to scream back.

Instead, she flipped over and threw the covers aside, enjoying the relatively cooler air that caressed her too warm body. All too soon, goosebumps pimpled her skin and she was chilled. Her choices were limited: draw the covers over her again or get up.

She got up.

Bel stood in the middle of the room, but she didn't know what to do. A month had passed since her break-up with Rick Mitchell. They'd dated for nearly five years, then Rick moved in last summer. Big mistake. You really didn't know someone until you lived with him. And it was easier to catch him cheating. How many times had he cheated the past five years? She hadn't asked him because she didn't really want to know.

Still chilled, Bel drew on her winter housecoat of thick flannel over silk short pajamas. All of her sleepwear was made of silk, her one indulgence. She loved the feel of cool silk slipping across her skin. Flannel was for warmth. She tied the belt and pulled hunters socks on her feet.

She missed Rick. Or the Rick she thought he was instead of the Rick he revealed himself to be. How does a woman spend over fifty percent of her free time with a man for five years and not know him? One of life's eternal mysteries, she thought as she padded down the hall to the kitchen. At least she hadn't married the jerk.

They'd talked about it, half-heartedly planning it for a few years down the road. She'd taken it seriously but Rick had obviously been patronizing her. He'd been crushed when his wife told him she was in love with another man, broken-hearted when he realized there was no chance of a reconciliation, and devastated by the divorce. Rick told her all this with a straight face and she believed him. Now, she wondered. Had his wife gotten fed up with his wandering ways and called it quits? It seemed a more likely scenario.

Bel jerked open the refrigerator door, the light almost blinding her. She would grab something to drink, then veg out in front of the TV. She couldn't decide if she wanted hot cocoa or cold boiled custard. She'd picked up a quart jug at the store after work, the only concession she'd made to the holiday season this year.

"Bah, humbug!" she said aloud.

What was the point? She had no family, no one to share Christmas with this year. Her brother and his family were in California, but she couldn't afford the trip yet. She had a cousin that she was somewhat close to, but this was her first Christmas with her new husband. Bel couldn't barge in on *that*. So why decorate? Why bake? Why make boiled custard from scratch? Why celebrate Christmas at all?

Bel decided on boiled custard because it would require effort to make hot cocoa. And she would forego her favorite holiday movies—*A Christmas Carol, Holiday Inn, and Christmas in Connecticut*—tonight and every night until Christmas. She wouldn't watch *It's A Wonderful Life* on New Year's Eve because in Real Life there was no hope. You didn't plan to jump in a river to end the misery only to be saved by an angel who showed you how wonderful your life really was.

Bel felt the tears begin. She didn't think she had any tears left. She thought she'd cried out all her tears over the split with Rick, and then the anniversaries of her parents' deaths. To top it all off, she would turn 30 in a couple of weeks. But here they were, burning the backs of her eyes, blurring her vision. She wasn't at the point where she was ready to dive into the Mississippi, but she was quite unhappy with her life. She pressed the heel of her free hand against her eyes, one at a time, clearing them of tears, and heard a thunk against the house.

Bel froze, listening. She couldn't tell where it had come from. Was someone trying to break in? If so, they were being very clumsy.

Then came a rolling rumble, a series of thumps and bumps, and now she could tell it came from the roof. Bel released the refrigerator door, plunging the room into darkness. She sniffled once and finished wiping her eyes. Suddenly, there was one more short rumble and a final, solid *thud* as whatever had toppled from the roof hit the ground.

Gradually, her eyes adjusted to the dimness. Moonlight and starlight filtered through the curtains. She sniffled as she eased aside the curtain on the door, but she couldn't see anything out of the ordinary, nothing moving in the shadows.

Stillness. Silence.

Suddenly, Bel thought of the old oak tree that had shaded the house from the front yard for decades. One of the huge branches might have snapped off. Or maybe the entire tree had fallen. She grabbed the flashlight from the nearest cabinet and opened the door.

Bel decided against turning on the outside light. It would spotlight her, and she wouldn't be able to see beyond the circle of light—just in case someone was out there. She dashed outside and around to the front of the house, flashing the light at the big oak. She didn't see a gaping hole in the lacework of branches, didn't see a fallen branch anywhere. The whole tree was still standing, straight and tall and starkly leafless against the night sky. If not the oak, then...

Back to the burglar theory. But why would someone be climbing on the roof when there were plenty of windows and doors to gain entry? All securely locked, of course, Bel reminded herself as she casually made her way back to the kitchen door. She saw no reason to panic and break into a wild run, alerting the would-be thief she knew he was there.

So far it had been a mild winter. While the night air was chilly, it was well above freezing. Still, she sniffled a few times, the chill air adding to the runny nose that her almost-crying jag had started. Over the sniffles, she heard another sound—a low moan.

Automatically, Bel shone the light in the direction from which it came. Her mother's rock garden spread along the side of the house like a flowerbed. Her mother had always collected rocks, large and small, everywhere she went, even from the decorative beds in front of her favorite restaurants and shops, to Bel's embarrassment.

In the center of the rock garden lay a man.

Bel gasped, then clamped a hand over her mouth. She couldn't believe there really was a thief, but there he was, sprawled amid the collection of rocks and stones. Bel flashed the light over him from head to toe. No movement. Was he breathing? She held her own breath, unable to do anything about the mad pounding of her heart, and watched him. After a few moments, she could see the shallow but steady rise and fall of his chest.

She should call 911, but what if he was bleeding to death? A few minutes could be the difference between life and death. She took a few steps toward him. What if it was a trap? To lure her closer so he could grab her and do who-knew-what to her. She stopped.

Examining him in the bright beam, she didn't see any spreading stain of red anywhere. Then his face caught her attention and she couldn't believe how gorgeous he was. Long black hair tangled around his face, and thick black brows swept over his eyes then slightly angled upward. His eyes were closed, long lashes smudging beneath. They seemed almost too large, yet they fit perfectly with the rest of his long, oval face—high cheekbones, long straight nose, full sensuous lips. *Kissable lips*, Bel thought then shook herself.

He was a burglar, or worse, and she was drooling over his lips.

He was an injured man who needed help, and she was drooling over his lips.

Either way, she was drooling — figuratively — and she needed to do something.

She flashed the beam along the length of his body from broad shoulders tapering to a cinched-in waist and legs that seemed to go on forever. At least six feet tall, she guessed. Yet the clothing he wore was too loose on him. The clothing...

Bel stepped closer. Unbelievably, he was wearing an elf costume. The Christmas-green suit had triangular points hanging from the tunic. A small red tote bag, gathered at the top, was tied to his belt. He even wore pointed elf shoes. She had never seen anyone more ill-suited to be an elf! What was he doing here, dressed like that? Where had he come from?

From the roof, she remembered suddenly. She straightened and shone the light up at the top of the house, but she didn't see anything. And what did she expect? A helicopter straddling the ridge? Or a sleigh and eight tiny reindeer?

She dropped the light to shine on him again. No blood that she could see. None of his limbs were twisted grotesquely, indicating a broken bone. He'd been knocked out cold so there could be a concussion. She really should call 911 and get the sheriff and an ambulance on the way.

But just as she made the decision to do so and took a step toward the kitchen door, he moaned again and moved. Bel quickly flashed the light over him. He was stirring, long legs bending, and one hand reached up to the back of his head as he raised a little. Bel stepped back, then ran into the kitchen.

Frantically, she jerked open the closet door. It was a large closet, a pantry really, but for now she used it to store the things that Rick had left behind. He had managed to accumulate an enormous amount of junk in the six months he had lived here and hadn't bothered to take it all with him.

The baseball bat was at the back, of course. She kicked boxes out of the way and grabbed it, then ran back outside. The giant elf hadn't moved much more, but both hands were at the back of his head now.

"Stay right where you are!" Bel shouted at him. "Don't move! I have a baseball bat and I know how to use it."

His head cocked to one side, but Bel didn't think she should count that as a movement. She really couldn't imagine having to bash the bat into that gorgeous face. She hoped he had a really good excuse for falling from her roof in the middle of the night.

One eye opened, then the other. He looked up at her and grinned, and she almost melted. Good grief, what a smile! Those full lips sort of tip-tilted up at one corner.

"Belinda? Belinda Cooper?" he asked. His voice was husky and shaky. From the fall, she supposed.

"H-How do you know my name?" she whispered, tightening her hold on the bat...and the flashlight. She was holding both, so she wasn't sure which she gripped harder.

"Santa Claus knows everyone's name," he said with a laugh, as if it was something she should know. He tried to rise on one elbow. "Santa Claus sent me. I'm Jingle, your Christmas Elf." Then he frowned and looked her up and down. "You're much smaller than I thought you'd be."

Before she could frame a reply to his crazy talk, he slumped back down and groaned, then didn't move again.

Her Christmas elf?

Now, Bel knew she had truly lost her mind. She had gone stark raving mad. Jingle, her Christmas Elf. What would she conjure up next: her own private tooth fairy, a pet Easter bunny, Elvis?

Bel let the end of the bat drop, grateful she hadn't called 911. What harm could an imaginary elf do? She crept closer to him, mesmerized by the perfect blending of imperfect features to create the best looking man she'd ever seen. No wonder he was so handsome and tall. She wouldn't have hallucinated a short, ugly elf.

He stirred again, blinking his eyes open. Bel directed the light so that it wouldn't be in his eyes, but she could still see him. Tentatively, she reached out and poked him in the side. He felt solid enough. But then wouldn't her cracked mind allow her to think so? She really didn't know how hallucinations worked. She'd never been confronted with one before.

"Why are you here?" she asked, more of herself than him, but he answered anyway.

"I told you, Santa sent me."

"Yes, that's what you said," Bel agreed. "But you're not real, y'know. Or at least I know it, and since I made you up, you should know it, too. Now, why don't you just disappear like a good little elf so I can finish having my breakdown in peace."

His black brows knitted in a frown, and his gaze swept over her briefly. Then one brow arched in a universal gesture of superiority. "I'm bigger than you."

"So you are. Which only proves you're not real. Elves are short, tiny little—"

"But I am short!" he interrupted forcefully. "I'm the smallest elf of all of Santa's elves. Are you the smallest human of all?"

And the thing was, Bel noticed in dismay, he asked the question seriously. What was worse, she answered him seriously.

"No. Actually, I'm quite tall for a woman—but I'm not the tallest either." She drew in a deep breath. "Look, this is insane. I'm sitting here in the middle of a rock garden with a giant elf. You're not real and I'm cold."

"Of course I'm real," Jingle said softly. He raised up suddenly, and before Bel could react, one arm had wrapped around her and his mouth closed over hers.

The kiss took her breath away—figuratively. His lips moved softly over hers and she responded without a second thought. She was only vaguely aware of his other hand brushing aside her hair, his fingers tracing the outline of her ear then rubbing back and forth across the top.

Shivers raced through her body, but she didn't know if from the cold or his kiss. When her belly tightened and heat stirred between her thighs, she pulled away from him, startled. Definitely the kiss.

"If-If you are real," she said, scrambling to her feet, "then you're crazier than I am. I don't know if hallucinations get cold, but you'd better come inside."

Bel hurried back into the house. If he was real, and he certainly felt real enough, she had just foolishly invited a stranger into her house. She flipped the switch, flooding the kitchen with light, and put the flashlight away. She held onto the baseball bat.

She hadn't realized how cold she was until she stepped into the warmth of the house. Her toes were numb and her fingertips were like icicles when she touched her skin. Strange, but she didn't remember his fingers being cold when he fondled her ear.

Jingle stepped into the doorway, broad shoulders filling it up, then he was inside, closing the door behind him. If he was the shortest and smallest elf of all, she didn't want to think about the size and stature of the rest of them!

He was over six feet tall, perhaps six-two or -three, which meant he was four or five inches above her own height. Tall men, she'd learned early on, didn't want tall women. They wanted petite. Short men, on the other hand, flocked to tall women. She'd never been comfortable looking down at a date, although she'd had several of those in the past. It was no wonder she'd imagined a tall elf. And dark skin. Could you really get a tan at the North Pole at the height of summer that would last year-round? Nah, she didn't think so.

"Can't Santa afford elfsuits that fit?"

Bel couldn't be sure, but she thought he blushed.

"The uniforms," he said quietly while tugging at his tunic, "don't come in my size."

She frowned. If she were going to conjure up an elf, she would have made his uniform more form-fitting, showing off the fantastic physique she'd no doubt given him. Unless it was somehow symbolic of her own insecurities. She wasn't a psychiatrist, but she could see the implications. She didn't wear her life well, so her imaginary elf's clothes didn't fit either.

The elf, something small and insignificant, represented her fractured psyche. His height and handsomeness because she was lonely and alone. She missed Rick more than he deserved. She thought she just missed having *someone* around. An elf was better than no one, she supposed, and set the bat side.

So much for psychobabble. She'd analyzed everything as well as she could, but Jingle was still here. *Jingle*! She was certain she should have come up with a better name than that.

Jingle was still rubbing the back of his head as he gazed around the kitchen.

"Sit down and let me look at your injury," Bel offered.

Jingle obediently sat in one of the kitchen chairs, and Bel walked up behind him. She wove her fingers into the glossy black waves and gently felt his scalp. A small bump, no larger than a walnut, bulged a little. That was good. If the wound had been sunken in, that would have been bad.

He didn't say anything or flinch from her touch, so she decided he wasn't hurt too badly. Since he was a figment of her imagination, did it matter?

"Do you feel dizzy or anything?" she asked just to be polite, although she couldn't quite justify being polite to a hallucination.

"No, nothing."

"Good. I was about to have some boiled custard. Do you want some? Or would you rather have hot cocoa?"

"Boiled custard?" he asked and turned to look up at her.

His eyes were the palest blue she'd ever seen, so pale as to be almost colorless. They stood out starkly against the tan of his skin and coal black hair.

"Kind of like eggnog," Bel explained as she took two cups from the drainboard and got the quart jug from the refrigerator. "Except it's thicker and no spice."

He watched her pour, then took the cup she handed him. He sipped, then broke into a delightful grin that almost made her heart stop beating. She'd certainly dreamed up the best-looking man she'd ever seen. Too bad he was an elf. Too bad he was imaginary.

"Reindeer Milk!" he said, surprised, and drained the cup.

"Reindeer milk? No, it's made with—"

"Mrs. Claus makes it, using reindeer milk, of course. She calls it her Special Reindeer Milk. Hers is thicker."

"Well, this is made with plain old cow's milk." Bel held up the jug. "More?"

He nodded eagerly and held out his cup. Bel refilled it.

When they'd finished, she looked at the empty cups sitting side by side and the nearly empty jug. Could an imaginary elf actually consume anything? Of course, a shrink would say she'd drunk it herself, but she certainly didn't feel like she'd had over half a quart of boiled custard. She set the jug in the fridge, and turned to find Jingle standing right behind her.

"I can't believe how small you are," he said, looking down at her.

No one had ever said *that* to her. "I-I'm not small. I told you before."

"But humans are supposed to be—" And he cocked his head back as if he was looking at the ceiling, then his pale blue eyes settled on her again. "On the television, in your Christmas movies, humans are always much bigger than elves, nearly twice as tall."

"I know. And since I've imagined you, I don't really know why you're not small."

He smiled that wonderful smile again, pleased. "Here, I'm not small at all, am I? But why do you think I'm not real?"

"Because elves aren't real," she explained. "Elves, whether Christmas elves or part of fairy tales, just aren't real. You can disappear now. I've decided I don't want to go crazy. It's too...too unsettling."

"How can you say I'm not real?" he asked softly and moved in closer. Bel tried to back away, but she was already against the refrigerator with nowhere else to go. He leaned in even closer, his full lips slightly parted, and he kissed her again.

Oh yes, he felt real. And so was the warmth that spread through her body. Feeling had come back to her fingers and toes because now they tingled. And that delicious burn in the pit of her belly, spreading lower... How long had it been since she'd been this easily aroused by a kiss? The kiss of a stranger. The kiss of an elf!

Bel pulled away violently, banging her head against the refrigerator. "No! You're not real. If you're real, then you're not an elf. If you are real, then you—"

"I'm real and I'm an elf," he said, keeping her pinned against the refrigerator, his body pressed to hers. Now she was all too aware of *his* arousal which only intensified her own. She almost missed the significance as he brushed his thick wavy hair behind one pointed ear.

Bel almost did a double-take. The top of his ear swept upward to a point. Not very high, she thought, unlike some pictures of elves she'd seen, because his hair had covered it completely. Almost like...

She reached up, thinking he'd done an fine job of attaching the piece. Not a seam or trace of makeup to be seen. She ran her hand along the peak which produced a deep sound in his throat. He closed his eyes, and his arousal pressed against her even harder.

"You can get these," she said, suddenly pinching the tip and twisting as hard as she could, "at any sci-fi convention!"

His eyes flew open and he yelped, thoughts of ecstasy fleeing mind and body, Bel noted with satisfaction. He grabbed at her hand, trying to free his ear, but Bel held on, determined to pull off the fake appliance. She held on, but so did the piece of rubber. What had he done, superglued the thing on?

"*Ow*! What are you doing? That *hurts*!" he yelled, struggling to get free of her vise-like grip. They crossed the kitchen until he was backed up against the counter. His face twisted in pain, he grabbed her arm and yanked it from his ear. She stared at the tip. It was beet-red but still firmly attached. She was forced to concede the pointed ear was real.

Unbidden, tears sprang in her eyes. If his pointed ears were real, then she really had lost her mind. She wrapped her arms protectively around herself and backed away from him.

"I don't know who you are," she whispered roughly, almost choking on the words as tears spilled down her cheeks. "I don't know *what* you are, but I want you gone. Now! I'm going to bed, and I don't want to see you again."

Bel whirled, grabbed the baseball bat, and ran from the kitchen before he could commence his silly ravings about how Santa Claus had sent him and he was her Christmas elf. In her bedroom, she closed the door and locked it. Then shoved a chair securely under the doorknob. Crawling into bed, she hugged the bat close to her. Poor substitute for a lover, she thought miserably, but she felt better with the weapon close by. Exhausted, she fell asleep almost instantly.

* * * * *

Brittle sunlight streamed through the window when Bel awoke to the fading echo of chimes. As she blinked her eyes open, the musical notes played several times in quick succession. She glanced at the clock. It read 1:00 and she had that uncanny feeling of *déjà vu*. She flung her hand aside to grab the covers...and felt a baseball bat in her bed.

Memories—no, memories of dreams, she corrected adamantly—rushed through her mind. She giggled. She had really dreamed up a Christmas elf named Jingle! The doorbell ran once more, and Bel scrambled out of bed, catching her robe and slipping it on as she went. She shook her head at the crazy dream as she moved a chair from under the knob and unlocked the door. She did not allow herself to think why the bat was in her bed or the door locked with a chair bracing it if it had all been a dream.

"I'm coming, I'm coming," Bel called out and hurried down the hall. She opened the door to find Violet Ramsay, an acquaintance from the office. Their desks were next to one another, but while the two were friendly toward each other, they had never associated outside the office.

Violet smiled and held out a familiar coffee mug. "You left this on your desk, half full of coffee. I brought it home and washed it. I figured by the time we came back after the holidays, alien lifeforms would have evolved."

Bel laughed and took the mug. The office was closed through Christmas and wouldn't reopen until after New Year's. "Thank you, Violet, but you didn't have to make a special trip out here —"

"I didn't. I mean, I was just going to bring it in to the office after the first, but I was coming out this way anyway. My great-aunt lives down the road a piece, so I thought I'd drop it off."

"I appreciate it. I don't know where my mind was yesterday."

"Anxious to get out of there, no doubt," Violet said with a grin. "Did I wake you?"

Bel nodded guiltily. "Yeah, I had one of those nights. I couldn't sleep. I tossed and turned for hours and when I finally did doze off, I had the craziest dream."

"I have nights like that, but the kids won't let me sleep late. They're always wanting something."

Violet shuffled in the cold. The temperature was in the 50's, and the sun was shining as brightly as it could in winter, but the breezy air had a snap to it. Bel could feel the chill curling around her ankles and drifting up her robe.

"I'm sorry. I don't know where my manners are. Come on in and I'll fix us some coffee."

Violet hesitated, then stepped inside. "I really shouldn't," she said as Bel closed the door. "I told Aunt Oscie I'd be right back, but coffee sounds good. That air is going straight through this sweater. I should have worn a heavier jacket, but it's so warm in the car with the sunshine."

"How is Miss Oscie? I haven't seen her in ages," Bel said as she led the way into the kitchen. "My grandmother and her were friends."

"Well, my grandmother is her sister. They don't get along, but I like to visit her occasionally. She's family and she does enjoy having the kids around. I keep telling Grandma she should try to patch things up, neither one of them are spring chickens, but Grandma and Aunt Oscie are both stubborn as mules."

Violet continued talking, something to do with both sisters being in love with the same boy. Violet's grandmother won. The two never spoke to one another again and Miss Oscie never married. Bel listened as she put on water to boil and brought two mugs from the cabinet.

"Oh my! I see you've gotten over Rick quick enough."

Bel froze, one mug still in her hand, then looked at Violet standing by the window that looked out over the backyard. In a weak moment, needing someone to talk to, Bel had confided in Violet when she found out about Rick's other woman. Violet had been sympathetic and assured Bel she'd made the right decision by throwing him out. Violet told her it wasn't a failing on her part, some men just couldn't grasp the concept of fidelity.

"Wh-What do you mean?" Bel stuttered, afraid of the answer.

Violet smiled and waved toward the window.

"Oh, didn't you know there's a man sunbathing in your backyard? In this weather! What is he, an Eskimo?"

Bel forced one foot in front of the other until she stood behind Violet. Her jaw dropped. The man from her dream, the *elf*, was getting up from a chaise lounge lawn chair. He walked toward the house. And he was shirtless!

The mug slipped from her fingers and hit the floor.

"N-No, not an Eskimo, but he is from up north," Bel said. After all, The North Pole was as far north as one could get.

"Where did you find him?" Violet asked, eyeing him appreciatively.

"Oh, he found me." Bel quickly scooped up the mug, which miraculously hadn't broken.

The truth slammed into her hard. She hadn't dreamed him up, and she hadn't imagined him. If Violet could see him, then Jingle the Christmas elf was real!

The kettle started to whistle just as Jingle came through the door. Bel scrambled to remove it from the burner and turn off the stove. Then she looked at Jingle. Oh yes, he had that fantastic physique she had imagined she would bestow upon a hallucination. Well-defined muscles corded his arms and chest. She'd never been one to go gaga over muscles, but she couldn't take her eyes off of him.

"Well, aren't you going to introduce us?" Violet asked.

"Sure," Bel said, startled. She'd forgotten anyone else was in the room—or in the world. "Violet Ramsay, a friend from the office. This is Jingle—"

"Alexander," he said at the same time.

Bel stared at him wide-eyed. He grinned, his gorgeous mouth tilting up at one corner, and shrugged a little, flexing quite a few of those muscles.

"Alexander," Bel conceded, thinking quickly. "Alexander is...a friend of...of my brother's. It's an old joke between us. Y'know, Jingle, Bel."

Violet laughed.

"He and my brother have been out of touch for awhile, and, uh, *Alexander*, didn't know that Shaun and his family had moved to California. When Alexander showed up today, I couldn't just turn him away."

"Of course not," Violet agreed. "It's nice to meet you, Alexander. But do you often sunbathe in the middle of winter?"

Jingle shook his head and Bel was relieved that his thick black hair didn't reveal the points of his ears with the movement. She could safely say he was from up north, explaining why this winter weather was mild to him, but there was no way to explain his ears. On the other hand, who in their right minds would believe he was an elf?

She did. But she still wasn't sure she was in her right mind even though Violet could see him, too.

Jingle was saying, "No, this is warm compared to The North—"

"I told Violet you're from up north," Bel interrupted. "Way up north."

Jingle nodded. "Yes. The north. This is warm compared to the north where I'm from."

"Okay," Violet agreed, eyebrows raised, and took the coffee mug from Bel. She helped herself to the creamer and sugar Bel had set out.

Forcibly tearing her eyes away from Jingle, Bel brought out another mug and handed it to him. Biceps flexed as he held out his arm to take it.

"You drink coffee, don't you?" Bel asked.

Jingle nodded. He took a sip, his nose wrinkling. She poured in creamer and sugar. When he sipped again, his nose didn't wrinkle quite as badly.

Bel took his arm and steered him toward the table. "It's instant, okay."

She watched him as, muscles rippling with every movement, he sat across the table from Violet. And Violet, she noticed, couldn't keep her eyes off of him either. Time to cover him up. Bel could do that. Without a word, she went into the pantry/closet and rummaged through Rick's stuff. She pulled out a wrinkled t-shirt. Jingle was bigger than Rick, but it should fit.

Back in the kitchen, she casually tossed the shirt at Jingle, then sat at the table with her coffee.

"Jingle's luggage was lost at the airport. It's an old shirt that Rick left behind," she explained to Violet.

Jingle finally managed to pull the shirt on, but Bel stared at him in dismay. He looked even sexier with clothes, than without them. The t-shirt was a bit too tight and every wrinkle vanished. The thin knit material molded to every muscle group, defining each line and curve deliciously. Violet could hardly drag her eyes away from the bulging biceps, the turgid triceps, the distended deltoids, and an intro to a perfect six-pack.

What struck Bel was that Jingle was completely unaware of the effect he had on both women.

"Well," Violet finally said a bit breathlessly. "I really should be going. I'm sure Aunt Oscie is wondering what's keeping me."

"You could always give her a call," Bel suggested.

"No, I'm sure the kids are getting too rambunctious by now. Nice to meet you, Alexander." Violet stood and with a last long glance at Jingle, or rather his fine physique, she turned to flee.

"It was nice to meet you, too," Jingle said politely and returned his attention to the coffee.

Violet stopped at the kitchen door so quickly that Bel almost ran into her.

"You will be at the Christmas party tonight, won't you?"

"No, I—" Bel began.

"Why don't you bring Alexander?" Then Violet turned to look at the hunk in question. "You will come, won't you?"

"I wasn't planning—" Bel started.

"A Christmas party?" Jingle stood and came around the table to stand beside Bel. "Will there be lots of laughter and good spirits?"

Bel didn't like the way his blue-white eyes had lit up. Surely, he didn't think to attend in his elf get-up?

Violet looked puzzled. "Sure. *Lots* of spirits. It's BYO. And snacks. I'm bringing my famous cheese dip."

"The kind that's spicy enough to peel paint?"

Violet laughed good-naturedly. "Yeah. I'll see you both tonight, then?"

Bel was cornered. Jingle seemed eager to go, and she could hardly disappoint her Christmas elf. She had really been looking forward to a quiet Saturday night at home. She would pop a big bowl of popcorn and settle down for the premiere showing on an overpriced movie channel.

When Violet had gone, she whirled on Jingle, but he had returned to his chair, sipping the coffee again. He made a face. "This tastes funny."

"It's instant. Get over it."

"Why don't you want to go to the party?"

Bel frowned and shrugged. "And spend even more time with people I have nothing in common with? Violet is all right. I guess she's the best friend I have at the office, but the rest of them..."

"Why don't you like them?"

"It's not that I don't like them. It's just that none of them share my interests, that's all. I have no need to listen to them talk about the things they like and they wouldn't be interested in what I enjoy. Even Violet. She's married, has children. I—I've never been married and no kids, so I don't know what it's like. My eyes tend to glaze over whenever she starts one of her cutesy stories about—"

"Why aren't you married?" he interrupted, asking the question innocently.

Bel shrugged, felt herself blushing. "I haven't found the right guy, the man I want to spend the rest of my life with."

Suddenly, she realized it was true.

"But there was a man, wasn't there?" Jingle asked, his voice low and thoughtful as he plucked at the shirt.

"Yes, there was Rick. You're wearing his shirt." Bel reached out and ran one finger down the center of his chest. Rick had never filled out the shirt the way Jingle the Christmas elf did. "But he wasn't the one."

Jingle caught her hand and pressed it against the center of his chest. He was warm and firm through the knit material. "How did you know?"

"We dated for five years and had some good times together. He even moved in for awhile and—and we talked about getting married. But..." Bel bit her lip. She didn't want to tell him Rick's cheating and leaving hurt her, not because she was desperately in love with him, but because she was alone again. "I think I knew from the beginning. I didn't feel it *here*." She tapped her fingers against his chest. "I didn't feel it in my heart."

He smiled and laid both hands over hers, entwining his fingers with hers. She had to turn the subject away from Rick. She didn't want to talk or even think about him.

"What about you? Is there a pretty elf maid waiting for your return to The North Pole?"

His smile dissolved into a frown. "No one waits for me."

"What about family? Your parents, brothers or sisters?"

He shook his head. "My parents are—gone. I have no brothers or sisters."

"My parents are gone, too. I have a brother, Shaun. He's married and they have two children, a girl and a boy. They moved to California early this year."

He perked up. "California? That's where *Baywatch* is."

"Yeah, but the show isn't being made anymore."

"I know that, but the beaches and the water and the sun are still there, aren't they?"

"Oh! You want to go to California. Me, too. I can't afford the trip yet, but I'm saving up. I'll stay with my brother, so I won't have to worry about a hotel. But there's the plane ticket and I want to make sure I have plenty of money for shopping and sight-seeing."

Bel had withdrawn her hands from his chest in her enthusiasm. Which was just as well. Touching him was not a good idea, not really. It made her want to do things she shouldn't do...like seduce an elf.

"Why are you here?" she suddenly blurted out. "You said Santa sent you, but you never said why."

"I'm supposed to help you regain your Christmas spirit. Santa is worried about you."

"About me? There are millions of people in the world. Why would Santa concern himself with me?"

"He told me you always left the best cookies he's ever eaten."

Tears sprang into her eyes. "I always thought Daddy ate them. Mama would spend hours in the kitchen baking cookies. I always helped, but I think I was more of a hindrance than a help."

"And you never asked for more than you really wanted."

"I never really wanted much."

"So Santa sent me to cheer you up. The first thing is to go to the Christmas party tonight. Parties raise everyone's spirits, don't they?"

"Look, Jingle—or Alexander. Which should I call you?"

"Alexander is my real name, but it's not an elf name. Jingle isn't a proper name here, is it?"

"No, it's not a common nickname."

"But I like it when you call me Jingle."

"Then it'll be Alexander in public and Jingle in private. As I was saying, I don't really want to go to this party."

"But I want to go. I've never been to a Christmas party."

"You don't have Christmas parties at The North Pole?"

"I mean, one for humans."

"Sometimes they're not very pleasant. People drink too much and say and do things they usually don't say or do in front of people they have to work with the rest of the year." Jingle looked so dejected, Bel gave in much too easily. "All right, we'll go, but we won't stay long. The first thing is to get you some clothes."

Bel managed to come up with an old pair of Shaun's jogging pants that didn't look too short with a pair of boots that had belonged to her father she'd found tucked away in her mother's closet. The shopping trip went well. It put a large dent in her California Dreamin' Fund, as she called it, but was well worth the effort.

Now dressed in a charcoal gray sweater, black jeans, and black boots, with his glossy black hair and startling pale blue eyes, Jingle turned heads when they stopped for something to eat. Even the waitress drooled over him.

Back at the house, they barely had time to shower and dress, but Bel took her time. Normally, she didn't bother with make-up, but she'd bought a few things and carefully applied the cosmetics. She pinned her hair up and let little wisps frame her face.

She wore a silk dress in midnight blue she'd bought several years ago and worn only once. Rick had given her an Austrian crystal jewelry set their first Christmas together. The crystals sparkled brighter than diamonds, and she didn't have to worry about losing them. Then she raided her mother's closet again for a sparkly shawl someone had give her years ago, but her mother had never worn.

When she came into the living room, Jingle was waiting for her. He looked yummy in the black slacks, vest, and jacket, and open-collar white shirt. Bel had a sense of time standing still as they just looked at one another.

Bel's breathing quickened and she grew warm all over. They could have a much better time if they stayed home, she thought. She remembered his kisses from the night before, eager, tender yet filled with passion and promise. They had taken her by surprise.

Now, she wished he would kiss her again with the same spontaneity because she couldn't imagine taking the initiative, kissing him until their lips hurt, sliding the jacket, vest, shirt, and slacks from his body, raising her arms as he pulled the dress from hers...Well, maybe she could *imagine* it, but she couldn't see herself actually doing it.

Jingle walked toward her and her heart hammered in her chest. But all he did was raise his bent arm to her in an elegant gesture.

"You look beautiful, Belinda."

No man had ever told her that before. Not even Rick when she'd worn this dress before. He had been waiting for her, too, pacing impatiently. When she came into the room, he'd snapped at her that they were going to be late, then charged out the door. Now, she couldn't even remember where they'd gone that night.

Why had she put up with his crap for so long? She had known even then why: she was afraid of being alone.

"Thank you," she said, tears threatening to ruin her eyes. She blinked them back. "You look nice, too."

He smiled, but shrugged and pulled at his collar. "It's different from the uniform."

Bel drove them to the party, and Jingle turned heads once again as they walked into the room. The women ogled, the men frowned. Violet and her husband Dave were the first to approach them.

"Dave, you remember Belinda Cooper, and this is Alexander..." Violet raised her eyebrows in question. She wanted a surname. Bel glanced at Jingle, but he looked blank. He hadn't mentioned a last name. Did Christmas elves have last names?

"Alexander...Elf, um — Elphberg." Bel pulled the name from a novel she'd read years ago. "Alexander Elphberg, an old friend of my brother's."

The office floozies, Teri and Lori, quickly cornered Jingle, but whenever Bel glanced their way, his blue-white eyes met hers and his gorgeous smile was only for her.

Bel sipped ginger ale as she mingled. She would be driving and alcohol usually hit her fast and hard. She nibbled at the food, avoiding Violet's hot-as-hell cheese dip. She'd forgotten to bring anything edible, but no one seemed to notice.

A couple of hours later, after Jingle had a chance to talk to everyone in the room with Teri and Lori sticking to his sides like Velcro, and she had managed to steer clear of Brad Benson's slurred innuendoes, Bel pulled Jingle free of the Cling-on warriors, saying she was ready to leave. She was surprised when he immediately agreed. Teri and Lori followed them to the door.

The cool crisp air was a relief after the stuffy atmosphere of the office.

At home, Bel showed Jingle her brother's old room. She had no idea where he'd slept the night before, probably the couch. She changed into silk pajamas and flannel robe, and washed her face free of make-up. She was plain old Belinda A. Cooper again.

In the kitchen, she put the kettle on. It wasn't very late, but she'd eaten enough at the party. All she wanted was a cup of coffee and to crash in front of the TV until she fell asleep. Her normal Saturday night routine, which had not been disrupted by Rick's moving in. Hadn't he spent every Saturday night with his friends, just as he'd done when they were merely dating? Why had she expected it to be different afterwards?

The phone rang, startling her. It was Elaine Grogan, whom she'd seen earlier at the party.

"Hi, Belinda. What a nice young man your friend is." Elaine was well into her fifties.

"Alexander, yes, he is nice. He's an old friend of my brother's, but had lost touch with him. He didn't know Shaun had moved away when he showed up here to visit."

"So you told me. Alexander and I had a little chat this evening. It was so generous of him to donate twelve dozen cookies to the bake sale we're holding next week for the Children's Fund. If y'all could have them at the community center bright and early Monday morning—"

"Twelve *dozen*?" Bel asked, disbelief making her voice go up an octave—or two.

"He said you had a wonderful recipe called Santa's Favorite."

"Yeah." Bel was at a loss for words. *Twelve dozen.*

"If they're as good as Alexander says they are, they should sell well."

"I'm sure they will," Bel agreed, her voice now at its normal pitch.

Bel was hanging up the receiver when Alexander joined her in the kitchen. She took a deep breath.

"That was Elaine Grogan. It seems you and she had an interesting conversation tonight."

He had the grace to blush. "I was going to tell you about that. The cookies."

"Do you have any idea how long it's going to take to make twelve dozen cookies?"

Jingle thought a moment. "No. How long?"

"You mean you don't bake?" Bel heard her voice rising again.

He shook his head. "Mrs. Claus does all the baking at The North Pole. She always has plenty of cookies and fruitcake and strudel on hand for all of us elves."

"But these have to be made by Monday morning. It's been years since I baked cookies. I'm not even sure which cookies I set out for Santa. Mama always did lots of baking for Christmas." Bel plopped down in a chair and buried her head in her arms. "It will take all day."

"Did you have anything else planned for tomorrow?"

"No."

"Then you have plenty of time."

She raised her head and glared at him. Jingle was grinning broadly. "You mean," she growled, "*we* have plenty of time. Get ready for your first lesson in baking cookies!"

December 20

Bel poured over her mother's handwritten recipes and decided sugar cookies were the easiest to make. Sprinkled with red and green sugar, they would easily pass for Santa's Favorites.

The baking wasn't as bad as Bel had anticipated. And as long as one didn't count the three or four dozen they'd either burned or forgot to add the sugar—or both—mistakes were minimal. By late afternoon, they had more than twelve dozen Santa's Favorites cookies layered with waxed paper in various boxes and tins Bel found around the house. She had made three trips to the store because she'd underestimated how many batches they would ruin. Then Jingle decided they needed to bake a few extra dozen for themselves.

Bel had to admit Jingle did a wonderful job of helping, but then weren't Christmas elves experts at being "helpers"? Of course, he had started the flour fight, and they'd both wound up covered in white and laughing until their sides hurt.

As they went about their mixing, rolling, and cutting, Jingle had told her about his life at The North Pole—how all the other elves either ridiculed or shunned him because he was different, that he'd chosen the elven name Jingle for himself when they made fun of the human name Alexander, and when he at last realized Tinsel the elfess would never return his feelings. Bel felt honored that he would share so much of himself with her.

She told him she knew what it was like to feel lonely in a crowd, too. But it was of her own making, wasn't it? She had never volunteered to bake cookies when Elaine Grogan began her seasonal plans for the Children's Fund. Elaine campaigned all year long, but the closer it was to Christmas, the more generous people were. She always had fund-raising projects planned for the last few days before Christmas.

Christmas, Bel mused, opened everyone's heart more...except her own.

After she showered off the flour and slipped into bed, Bel grudgingly admitted Jingle's idea hadn't been too bad. She was exhausted and fell asleep quickly, sleeping the entire night through.

December 21

Bel woke early. Her arms and hands were sore from all the stirring the day before, but as she dressed, the aches eased somewhat. She wondered if Jingle was up yet. She stopped at the door to her brother's old room and knocked, then again. When Jingle didn't answer, she opened the door. The bed was neatly made, and she wondered if he'd even slept in it. He had promised to finish cleaning the kitchen when she'd gone to bed.

Bel closed the door and continued down the hall. When she entered the living room, she stepped into a winter wonderland.

Every table and shelf surface had been cleared of the everyday knickknacks and covered in twinkling, sparkling holiday decoration. Boughs and garlands of pine, dotted with gilded and glittered cones and festooned with red and white and gold bows, draped across the walls and mantle, windows and doorways. A huge wreath, stuffed with candy canes and ready to be hung, leaned near the front door.

In the center of the room, amid a snowscape of cotton on the cherry wood coffee table, sat the most beautiful nativity scene she'd ever seen. All the fancy crystal ornaments and expertly tied bows paled in comparison.

Bel dropped to her knees to examine the crèche. Each small board of the stable had been fastened individually to the frame. Every fold in Mary's and Joseph's robes and baby Jesus' swaddling cloth had been painstakingly detailed. Three shepherds herded a small flock of sheep, every curl of wool carefully carved, and three wisemen, bearing intricately cut coffers, sat on tasseled rugs atop their camels. An angel, every feather visible in her wings, hovered near a delicate star.

Bel almost expected the angel to take flight at any second, the star to shine its beacon on the manger, and the other pieces to move, playing out that magical night so long ago. She reached out, meaning to pick up a piece and examine it more closely.

Then Bel realized what made them lifelike, and she withdrew her hand in amazement. Different shades of wood had been used, sometimes many on one little statue. The star was created using a mixture of a dozen or more light colored woods. The swaddling cloth was entirely made of near-white wood. The beards and hair on every one was made of shades of brown and black. Looking even closer, Bel saw that each tiny iris was individually made from brown woods.

"It's all right," Jingle said from behind her. He lifted a shepherd and placed it in her hand. "You can look at them. They were made to be touched."

Bel ran her hand over the statue, the finish as smooth as silk. She squinted to see minuscule slivers of gray wood embedded in the brown wood beard and hair. Fine wrinkles were carved into the corners of his eyes, giving him a weathered appearance. Tiny toes peeked out from the edge of his robe, a darker shade of brown sandal strap across the foot. The detail was incredible.

"Where did you get this?"

Jingle shrugged. "I made it."

"You made it? When?"

"That's the work I do at The North Pole. Number Seven is the woodworking shop. Children these days don't care for old-fashioned wooden toys, so we make other things too. This is the first nativity I made. I brought it along with me, along with the decoration." His arm swept to the side, and Bel looked at the over-decorated room. She carefully set the shepherd in his place among the sheep.

"But where did you have them? You were unconscious when you fell off the roof into the rock garden."

"In one of Santa's bags." He found the little red tote bag and showed it to her. Bel remembered seeing it tied to his waist.

"You had all of this in *that*?"

Jingle nodded. "No one knows how they work, but that's how Santa carries all the toys."

Bel nodded. It wasn't her place to question the magic of Christmas. "It must have taken you a long time to carve these pieces and put together the stable."

Jingle shrugged. "Not very long. I finished this in half a day."

Bel laughed. "Yeah, but a 'day' is like six months at The North Pole, right?"

"I meant a work day. Elves work very quickly. I have some more things I thought I'd donate for the Children's Fund."

Jingle started pulling out more wooden items from the little red bag. One was a beautiful lantern with wooden flames licking upward from a half-burned candle with wax dripping down its side, all carved from a single block of wood. Others followed, each as extraordinarily detailed as the next. Bel was overwhelmed.

Jingle pointed to the last two—a miniature sleigh pulled by eight tiny reindeer with rows of jingle bells on the harness straps and a twelve inch tall pine tree decorated with the tiniest ornaments and candy canes, ropes of popcorn and berries, and lighted candles attached to the ends of branches. Bel ran her hand over the tree, each needle carved in exacting detail and sanded smooth.

"I just made these. I found the workshop out back yesterday when I was looking for a chair to sunbathe in. I hope you don't mind."

"You-You made these last night? Jingle, that's impossible!"

He looked hurt. "I told you, elves work quickly."

"I'm sorry. It's not that I doubt you, it's just that..." She took a deep breath. "Each one of these things would take months, maybe years for a human to make, even if he was a master woodworker. It's just hard for me to understand. But they're all beautiful. They should bring in a lot of money for the Children's Fund."

He seemed pleased at the prospect that his wooden carvings would help. "Do you really think so?"

"Yes, I really think so." Bel set aside the tree. "The workshop was my dad's. He liked to tinker around out there, building things, but he never made anything like this. He would make shelves and tables for Mama and us. Sometimes he'd sell things, but it was more of a hobby for him. Shaun kept up the shop until he moved to California. I haven't been out there since I stored the grill and lawn furniture late last summer."

"Then you don't mind that I used it?"

"Of course not, Jingle. Use it as long as you like."

"Only until Christmas Eve. That's when Santa will come for me," he quietly reminded her.

"Oh," Bel said and stood.

His words were as painful as a swift kick to her stomach. Jingle was her *Christmas* elf. No reason for him to stick around after the holiday was over. Santa had made a special trip to drop Jingle off on her roof, but it only made sense Santa would pick up Jingle as he made his rounds on Christmas Eve — only three days away. Three very short days if they passed as quickly as the last few.

"Well," Bel said, unable to imagine life without Jingle. "We'd better get your things and the cookies over to the community center." Then she glanced around at the abundance of holiday cheer in the room. "When we get back, we have to have a little chat about decorating."

Elaine and the others who were helping at the center were stunned by the beautiful pieces Bel and Jingle pulled out of the carefully packed boxes. They would have been speechless had Jingle brought the little Santa bag that defied space and gravity. One woman bought the lantern on the spot. Bel and Jingle stayed until mid-afternoon, after all the baked goods were gone and Jingle's crafts had all sold.

As Bel and Jingle headed out the door empty-handed, Lillian Vandell called after Jingle.

"Don't forget! Tomorrow night at 5:30."

"A date?" Bel asked with raised brow as they headed for the car.

"We're going caroling tomorrow night."

"Oh, we are?"

"Yes, it'll be fun," Jingle said, smiling his gorgeous smile that was only for her.

Bel didn't have the heart to dampen his enthusiasm. "Loads of fun," she agreed, keeping the sarcasm to a minimum.

December 22

A blustery cold front moved in overnight and Bel awoke to thickly frosted windowpanes. She and Jingle rearranged the decoration in the living room, spreading it out over other rooms in the house. She left the nativity scene on the coffee table.

After lunch, they went shopping again. If Jingle insisted on caroling in the colder weather, he needed a coat, gloves, scarf, and cap. They also bought groceries. Bel was running out of everything because she hadn't counted on feeding an extra person for a week.

Before going to bed the night before, Bel had planned a special menu. Since Jingle wouldn't be with her on Christmas Day, it would have to be Christmas Eve. His farewell dinner, Bel thought miserably, tears blurring the shopping list she'd made.

Bel had to dig deeper into her California Dreamin' Fund, but she didn't really mind. Instead of visiting her brother and his family next spring as she'd planned, she'd go next Christmas. She didn't think she could ever bear another Christmas alone in the house again. Too many memories of Jingle would remain.

She couldn't understand how important he had become in the few days he had been in her life.

They brought the last of the purchases into the kitchen on a gust of frigid air. Bel stumbled in and dropped her bags.

"My fingers are numb!" Of course, she had forgotten her gloves. She blew on her hands, trying to warm them up.

Jingle set down the bags he carried and closed the door. He reached out and took her hands in his. He hadn't put on his gloves yet, but his skin was warm next to hers.

"You're not even cold."

"I'm used to colder weather than this," he said, rubbing his hands briskly over hers.

This close to him, touching him, heated her all over, from the inside out. When he cupped his hands around hers and blew his warm breath on her fingers, she automatically snatched them away. She cleared her throat.

"I'm fine."

"No, you're not," Jingle said and lay a hand on her cheek. "Your skin is cold and it shouldn't be."

She didn't feel cold, not now. She'd kept as far away from his as possible while living in the same house with him the last few days. His kisses were too tempting —

As if he'd read her thoughts, his lips closed over hers, catching her by surprise. She responded naturally, her arms easing around his neck. He held her close to him, deepening the kiss, and she melted inside. She allowed herself only a few moments of the pleasure. Any longer and she wouldn't be able to say no.

Bel broke free of the kiss. She nuzzled against him, reveling in the feel of his lips against hers, then she looked up into his blue-white eyes.

"This isn't a good idea," she said.

"It feels like a good idea to me." Jingle smiled and touched her cheek again.

Her hand covered his and she pressed her lips against the tips of his fingers. "But it's not a good idea," she murmured.

"Why?"

Because he'd be gone by Christmas, but she wouldn't tell him that. He didn't belong in her world, nor she in his. The best thing she could do was pretend he'd restored her faith in Christmas so he could return to The North Pole satisfied he had accomplished his mission. Then she could get on with her life as empty as it was.

"Because we have too much to do." Bel said and pulled away from him. She lifted a bag to the counter and began taking out canned goods. "We have to put these away and get ready to go caroling. And please don't let anyone talk you into participating in any more festivities. I've had about as much Christmas spirit as I can stand."

"You haven't had fun the past few days?" Jingle asked warily.

Bel bit her lip. So much for pretending she was happy. She would have to do better. She plastered a bright smile on her face.

"Of course I have!" she said a little too eagerly. She toned it down. "Really, it's been fun. The office party wasn't as much of a drag as I'd thought it'd be. And I'm glad I helped at the community center. I'll probably do more volunteer work there. The caroling will be fun tonight. Too bad the weather didn't hold until afterwards."

Secretly, she was glad the weather had turned. The caroling would be cut short because of the bitter cold. It might be cancelled. She would call Lillian after they'd put up the groceries and find out.

Unfortunately, the caroling was still on, but the route had been shortened because of the colder weather. Bel made the best of it. The good thing was that some people offered them hot cocoa or hot Dr Pepper and lemon. It helped warm them up, but Bel was in painful need of a bathroom by the time they started for home. Jingle fell in love with the hot Dr Pepper and lemon and made Bel stop by a store and get some.

Back at home, after a quick supper of sandwiches, Bel showed Jingle how to make hot Dr Pepper and lemon. She popped in a tape of *Christmas in Connecticut*, one of her favorite holiday movies, as they sipped the hot, fragrant drink. Watching with someone who enjoyed it as much as she did was wonderful.

"A Christmas tree!" Jingle said when it came to the part in the movie where Barbara Stanwyck decorated the tree while Dennis Morgan played the piano and sang — one of Bel's favorite moments in the movie. "We need a tree."

Bel had to admit he was right. With the house decorated, a tree would be the final touch.

"All right," Bel agreed. "We'll get one tomorrow."

She was rewarded with one of Jingle's gorgeous smiles.

December 23

The next day was just as cold and blustery. After lunch, they went in search of the perfect tree.

Jingle rejected all the trees everywhere they went. It was nearly dark by the time they found a place on the highway. Jingle carefully examined every tree. At last, he found the one he wanted. It looked a little lop-sided to Bel, but she wasn't going to argue.

They carried the six-footer into the house and put it in the stand Bel had dug out of the utility room before they left. Jingle turned on the radio and Christmas music played softly in the background as they took their time getting it perfectly straight. With the uneven side toward the window, it was a pretty tree.

"Where's your little red bag?" Bel asked as soon as Jingle was satisfied with the placement of the tree.

Jingle looked up at her. "Why?"

"To decorate it, of course."

"I didn't bring any decoration for the tree."

"You brought all the other decoration. I thought you'd have some for the tree."

"Don't you have decoration for the tree, Belinda?"

"Yes," she said. "In the utility room, where the stand was."

"Why don't you get them?" he asked, but she felt like she was being pushed into something she didn't want to do.

She couldn't tell him she hadn't touched the Christmas tree decoration in the five years since her mother died. The first Christmas was much too soon. Bel was still in mourning. Even Shaun hadn't decorated his house much for Christmas. The second year was Bel and Rick's first Christmas together, and she was always at his place. After that, it was almost as if she was trying to see how long she could hold out.

"Okay," she said at last and retrieved the boxes.

The first box was marked "Lights" in her mother's scrawl. Most of the dozen strands worked, and they carefully wound them around the branches. The other two boxes were simply marked "Decoration". Bel opened one.

Inside were ropes of garland and all the handmade ornaments Shaun and she had made while in school—clothespin reindeer, cotton ball snowmen, and paper snowflakes. Bel laughed as she told Jingle which were Shaun's and which were hers. Most of Shaun's were crooked or only half-finished. They hung the ornaments on the tree as Bel told Jingle stories about Christmases when she was little.

In the last box were her mother's ornament collection. She had collected ornaments the same way she collected rocks.

"No matter where we went, Mama couldn't pass a gift shop without buying an ornament or a parking lot without picking up a rock. I remember Daddy teasing her mercilessly about both, but she would just laugh."

Unwrapping the ornaments, Bel felt tears prick her eyes. They brought back memories of the sound of her mother's voice as she told the story of where she'd gotten them. Bel couldn't remember them all, but she told Jingle the ones she could recall.

When the last ornament was hung, they tossed handfuls of icicles into the tree until the tip of every branch was laced with silver strands. Then Bel turned off the overhead light and Jingle plugged in the tree lights.

The room filled with a soft twinkling glow, and Bel stared at the tree. She remembered Christmases past when her life was filled with family and fun. And Christmases present when it was all she could do to get through the season without sinking into depression. And Christmases future?

She could imagine Jingle staying here with her. He could use the workshop and sell his extraordinary wooden crafts to earn a living. There could be laugher and fun in her future, if only...

Jingle was handing her a cup of hot cocoa. She blinked and took it. Christmases future would be without Jingle. He was leaving Christmas Eve, tomorrow night. Would he stay if she asked? The words were on the tip of her tongue, but she couldn't get them out. She sipped cocoa instead. Jingle turned off the Christmas music, and she put on a tape of *Holiday Inn*.

December 24

Christmas Eve

Bel spent the afternoon cooking. After lunch, she shooed Jingle out of the kitchen and told him she was best left alone. She could only hope dinner would turn out well. She hadn't really cooked in a long time, relying on fast food and frozen dinners for far too long.

It was late when she called Jingle in to get dressed for dinner. She had meant for them to have an early dinner, but everything took longer to prepare than she thought. She had spread the dining table with white linen and used the good china. She had just struck a match to light the candles when Jingle came in. He was dressed in his elf uniform. Bel froze and the flame went out.

Jingle saw the look on her face and self-consciously tugged on his tunic. "I know it doesn't fit right, but I thought I might as well wear it. Santa comes tonight."

A knot of pain tied in her stomach. Santa would come tonight to take Jingle away, not leave anything beneath her tree. It wasn't fair! Angrily, she struck another match. Jingle was *her* Christmas elf. Santa had given him to her. Why was he taking him away? Santa wasn't supposed to take back presents!

Bel knew she was being unreasonable. Jingle wasn't a toy or scarf or piece of jewelry. He was a person, even if he was an elf. He couldn't be given to her to keep, not really. Just like Cinderella couldn't keep her fairy godmother or — or...She was babbling to herself and that wasn't good.

"Are you all right?" Jingle asked, walking around the table toward her.

"Yes, I'm fine." Bel walked away from him, around the other side of the table, to lay the matches on the sideboard. "Please sit and we can eat. I hope you like it. I don't really cook much, so this was an experiment."

They sat and ate. Jingle complimented her on how good the food was. Bel thought he was humoring her because everything was as tasteless as straw to her. She nibbled and listened to Jingle trying to make small-talk, but gave monosyllabic responses. She was ruining their last day together, but she couldn't seem to help herself. She didn't want him to go. She didn't want to be alone again. No, it was more than just not wanting to be alone. She didn't want to lose Jingle.

"When will he be here?" She blurted out the question suddenly, interrupting Jingle. But he knew whom she was talking about.

"Sometime during the evening. I'm not sure when."

He threw down his napkin and Bel took that as a sign he was through. So much for a cozy, candlelit dinner for two, she thought as she began clearing away dishes. Jingle helped her.

"I'm not looking forward to telling Santa that I failed," he said as they placed the dirty dishes in the sink.

Guilt washed over Bel. She had forgotten she was supposed to pretend to be full of Christmas spirit. But how could she even pretend when her Christmas elf would be leaving? She turned on the faucet to fill the sink with water.

"You didn't fail," she said and squirted dishwashing liquid under the rush of water. "I've had more fun this

Christmas than I have in a while. I'm glad you came and made me do Christmasy things. I know I'm not bubbling over with holiday joy, but I'm a little out of practice. Santa will know, won't he? He'll know I'm trying."

Jingle sighed in relief. "Yes, he'll know."

They washed dishes and put away the food. Jingle made them hot Dr Pepper and lemon and asked what movie Bel planned for this evening. The evening wasn't going as she thought it should, but she didn't know how to get it on track. She couldn't bring herself to ask him to stay. He hadn't indicated he wanted to stay.

Bel put on *A Christmas Carol* with Alistair Sim, which she liked better than the old black and white 30's version. She couldn't concentrate on the movie, was conscious of every second ticking by. The movie ended too quickly and it was ten o'clock. Two hours till midnight and Christmas Day. Tears burned her eyes. She excused herself and left the room. In her bedroom, she changed into a silk nightgown and flannel robe, tears spilling down her face. She washed her face, not wanting Jingle to see that she'd been crying.

Back in the living room, with only the twinkling Christmas tree lights on, instrumental Christmas songs played softly in the background. Jingle stood in front of the tree. She had taken no pictures of him! She quelled the urge to run for her camera. To have pictures to look at for the rest of her life but knowing she'd never see him again was unthinkable. She would carry Jingle in her heart.

Bel crossed the room to stand beside him.

"I thought you'd gone to bed without saying good-bye," he said.

"I'd never do that. I'll wait here with you." She paused a moment. "I'm going to miss you."

It was an opening, a way to let him know how important he had become to her without laying open her heart. If he chose, he could make the first move, say he would stay a while longer or at least ask her if she wanted him to stay. She watched him expectantly, his pale eyes twinkling with the glow of the tree lights.

"I'll miss you, too, Bel," he said taking a step toward her. Then she was in his arms, looking up at him. She was ready to accept what he could give her—this one night.

Jingle kissed her, tentatively at first his full, warm lips claiming hers. When Bel didn't pull away or make excuses but closed her eyes and readily accepted him, he drew her into his arms, deepening the kiss.

Bel tilted her head back and raked one hand through the thick waves of his hair, her fingers brushing his ear. He had made a sound of ecstasy deep in his throat when she'd fondled the tip that first night. Now, she found the point and stroked it, swirling her fingers over the strange, exotic peak. That same deep moan rumbled in his throat and his hips surged toward hers. She met him thrust for thrust, each contact sending a thrill through her.

"Is this a good idea now?" Jingle asked against her lips, his voice raw and husky.

"Yes. Yes, a very good idea," Bel whispered. He certainly felt adequately equipped, but she didn't know a thing about elf anatomy. "Do elves make love the same way humans do?"

"Uh-huh," he murmured.

"Oh, good." She slipped her hand between their bodies, cupping the hot bulge she found. She massaged him gently but firmly and was rewarded when he grew longer, larger, harder.

Time to get off their feet and on her back, Bel thought. She felt as if she could climb him right there, wrap her legs around him, and just do it—if clothes weren't in the way and the laws of physics didn't apply.

Bel tossed back her head and Jingled kissed along her throat, moving lower until he'd reached the top of her breasts. He pushed aside the bodice of her nightgown until one breast was free and it filled his hand. His head dipped lower, his mouth surrounding the nipple, his tongue caressing the hard peak. His other hand found her other breast, thumb brushing the nipple until it was a hard nub, and the intense sensations weakened her knees. The silk nightgown seemed to melt away as the heat of his hand branded her skin. Bel's body arched toward him, desire cascading through her. She wanted him, wanted him more than she'd ever wanted any man or elf. He eased the nightie down until it fell free, a cool silken puddle around her feet. It wasn't quite fair that she was naked and Jingle fully clothed. She groped for the points of his tunic and started pulling up.

He lifted his head and looked at her, and his blue-white eyes now darker with desire. He raised his arms and she stripped him of the over-large garment, baring the hard body she'd been trying to ignore. Dropping the tunic, she ran her hands over the smooth muscles, brushing fingertips over nipples that drew taut at her touch. She moved in closer to trail kisses from the center of his chest to the hollow of his throat. Her fingers hooked in the waistband of his pants and pushed down over slim hips and the bulge that had grown incredibly. Baggy elfsuits hid everything well. She couldn't resist trailing a kiss along one thigh.

Jingle wove his fingers into her hair and gently pulled her upright again. He stepped out of pants and shoes, then his lips met hers hungrily. He swept her up, one arm catching behind her knees. His warm skin felt silken next to hers and she sighed contentedly as their lips parted.

His pale eyes caressed her. "I want you, Belinda."

She didn't know whether to laugh or cry. Laugh at his stating the obvious. Or cry because no man had ever looked at her in such a tender way or said he wanted her and sounded as if he meant it with everything in him. Certainly, no man had ever swept her off her feet — literally. She did neither. Jingle wouldn't understand either reaction.

Instead, she smiled and ran a fingertip over his lips. "I want you, too."

"Are you sure? You've always turned away from me before." He sounded doubtful.

Bel feared he would set her on her feet and refuse to quench the fire he'd started within her. Tonight was her last night with him and she wanted it all. She brushed the hair away from his ear, trailing a finger along the peak and watched as his eyes closed and his expression mellowed with pleasure.

"The timing wasn't right," she leaned close and murmured into his ear. "And now it is. I want you, Jingle."

Her tongue took over and traced up to the point, then down again. Then she took the point into her mouth and suckled gently. Jingle's grip tightened around her, and he groaned. She turned his head and lavished the same attention on his other ear. She could feel his knees giving out beneath him, weakened by the passion she stirred in him.

Jingle carried her across the room and lay her on the broad sofa, her head and shoulders amid throw pillows. He joined her, lying by her side, his long limbs surrounding her.

They kissed and touched, exploring one another's bodies in the blinking lights of the Christmas tree. She tried to watch him in the ever-changing shadows, tried to read beyond his desire for her, but then he would caress her and make her gasp and lose all thought except that she wanted him to do it again or probe deeper or move faster.

By the time she had learned every curve of his supple body and he had discovered the places she liked to be touched, she quivered with need. His shaft was rigid and tremulous where it lay across her thigh. She grasp his length and stroked it. His hips undulated with the rhythm. His hand left her breasts and slid over her ribs and belly, fingers tangling in the patch of curls. Her legs automatically parted and she writhed against his delving fingers. Tingles of pleasure danced over her skin as he swirled around that most sensitive place, then plunged inside her, swirled and plunged, again and again. His mouth captured the sounds escaping her throat, as her body trembled with the release and she cried out. When the tremors in her body stopped and she relaxed, he withdrew his hand and moved over her. Her legs spread wide to accommodate his hips.

He thrust into her slick wetness gently, slowly, and she felt every inch of him enter her deeply. She wrapped her legs around him and he settled against her.

"You feel so good," he murmured and gathered her into his arms.

"So do you," she said on a sigh. "I think I wanted this from the moment you kissed me in the rock garden, even when I thought you were a burglar. Or my imagination."

His sensuous lips turned up in a smile. "I made my usual clumsy entrance that night. I was supposed to come down the chimney."

Bel wriggled against him. "Well, you didn't make a clumsy entrance tonight."

He pulled out until only the tip of him touched her. "Can I try it again, just to make sure?"

"Of course. Try as many times as you like. Practice makes perfect, y'know." Bel nudged toward him for encouragement.

Jingle took the hint and slid into her again. They found the rocking rhythm that felt best, and Jingle cradled his head on her shoulder, their bodies wrapped together like a small Christmas package.

Bel closed her eyes. She didn't think of how this would be their only night together and Jingle would be gone soon, whisked away by a sleigh, back to The North Pole where he belonged. No, he belonged here with her.

She'd actually fallen in love with her Christmas elf. *Thank you, Santa, for making my Christmas wishes come true...but how can you take him away again?* It was too late to write a letter to Santa, asking him to let Jingle stay.

How could she let him go? she thought for the thousandth time. But how could she beg him to stay?

Thoughts drifted away and the sensations inside her consumed her. Their movements came faster and faster until the sofa beneath them groaned for relief. Then the pleasure burst inside her and spread warmly through her limbs. Her back arched and she ground her hips against his, making it last as long as possible, until she could feel her toes again.

Jingle sprinkled kisses along her cheeks and lips. "Did it feel good?"

She nodded, breathless, unable to speak. She had grown used to his way of commenting on the obvious with complete sincerity.

He raised above her, head thrown back and back bowed, straining into her with short, hard thrusts. Then he stiffened and everything seemed to drain from him at once. He draped limply over her, mostly lying to the side to keep his weight off her. His breathing was labored.

Bel reached up and touched his cheek, brushing aside glossy strands of hair. He opened his eyes, pale blue-white almost glowing in the twinkling lights of the Christmas tree.

"Did you feel good, too?"

"Yes, very good. Better than I've ever felt."

"I'm glad I made you feel good," Bel whispered. *I'm going to miss you*, she wanted to say. *I don't want you to go. Please stay.* Even after their intimacy, she couldn't say the words. Instead, she nestled in the crook of his arm as he covered them with the blanket that lay over the back of the sofa.

She put her arm around his waist and lay her head on his chest. Maybe if she held him tight enough, Santa wouldn't be able to take him away.

Bel felt him place a kiss on her forehead and his hand fondled her hair. She meant to remain awake until Santa came, but cuddled in the comfort of his arms, she drifted off to sleep.

* * * * *

The noise on the roof woke Jingle. Belinda was snuggled close to his side. Her dark brown hair lay in a spray over his shoulder and across his chest. One arm hugged him, her body half over his, their legs entwined. He didn't want to move away from her, but it was time.

Easing away from her, he stood as she shifted and murmured in her sleep. Gently, Jingle brushed wisps of hair from her face, and she settled into the warmth he'd left behind.

He put on his pants and shoes. Just as he turned, Santa magically appeared from the chimney flue without singeing a whisker.

"Alexander!" Santa spoke softly, his eyes twinkling as he looked from Jingle to Bel and back to Jingle again. He tugged on his snow-white beard.

"Merry Christmas, Santa," Jingle greeted him, unsure how to tell him. "How is the trip going tonight?"

"Very good, very good. The new reindeer are flying smoothly." Santa paused. "And how have you been this past week?"

"Everything went well."

Santa looked around the room. "The decoration is festive. Did you succeed in raising Belinda's Christmas spirit?"

"Yes, I think I did. It'll take time, but I think Belinda will celebrate Christmas from now on."

"Yes, I believe you're right." Santa tugged his beard again. "Is there something you want to tell me, Alexander?"

Jingle nodded, still reluctant to tell Santa of his decision.

"Out with it, lad. I can't help you if you don't ask."

Jingle drew in a deep breath and took the plunge. "I want to stay! Here, they call me Alexander and no one laughs. No one ignores me or ridicules me. Everyone accepts me as I am. Bel's friends are now my friends — or they will be when we've had more time. And Bel..."

"And?" Santa prompted.

"I don't want to leave her. She knows exactly *what* I am and she still —" He broke off as he felt his face grow warm, remembering what they'd done before Santa arrived.

"You're a Christmas elf." Santa sighed heavily. "You know it's against the rules for any of the Christmas elves to leave Christmastown."

"I know, but I've never been accepted there. And I've certainly never been happy, not since my mother returned to the Elfland." Jingle drew in another deep breath and with it the courage to continue speaking. "I've never asked you for anything, Santa, not even a uniform that fit. But I am asking you to allow me to stay here with Belinda. It's the only Christmas wish I've ever had."

"If I allow it, there's no going back," Santa pointed out gravely. "If you stay, you can never return to Christmastown."

"I understand," Jingle said just as solemnly. "I'll miss you and Mrs. Claus, but it's what I want."

Santa stroked his beard as he considered the request. Jingle knew that even if Santa refused, he would not return. He had asked as a mere courtesy, out of respect for Santa.

"Very well, Alexander. If it's truly what you want—"

"It is," Jingle answered firmly.

"We'll miss you, the Missus and I, but maybe it is for the best." Santa clapped him on the shoulders. "I hope you find here what you've been looking for your whole life."

Jingle returned the embrace. "I don't think I've been searching for anything except acceptance. I've already found that here. Now, I just want a chance at a life with Bel."

"Good luck, lad."

"Thank you, Santa. Give my love to Mrs. Claus, and tell her thank you for everything."

Jingle watched as Santa magically disappeared up the chimney with "Merry Christmas! Ho, ho, ho!" fading in the distance.

A few seconds later, Jingle heard a clatter of hoofbeats on the roof, the tinkling of bells, and then silence. He turned to look at Bel.

He felt better than he had in a very long time. The only other time he'd ever been happy was with his mother, and that time was tainted with her melancholy. Twilight hadn't been happy, and he could never get her to tell him why.

Never seeing Santa or Mrs. Claus again made him sad, but he felt relief at never having to face Tinsel or Zap or any of the others. A chance for happiness with Bel was all he wanted.

He shed the shoes and ill-fitting pants and tried to slip back into place beside Bel without waking her. She stirred, looking up at him sleepily as she snuggled against him.

"Santa hasn't come yet?" she asked around a yawn.

Jingle ran his hand over her shoulder. "He came, but I...I told him I didn't want to go back."

Bel sat up quickly, a hopeful expression on her face. "And?"

"And Santa agreed."

"Oh, Jingle!" She threw her arms around him and hugged him tightly.

He released a sigh of relief. "Then you don't mind?"

She shook her head against him. "I wanted to ask you to stay, but I didn't know how. I didn't even know if you wanted to stay. I don't know what I would have done if you'd left."

Jingle drew the blanket up closer, then wrapped his arms around her. "I don't know if there's a future for us, but I knew I couldn't walk away from it."

"I think if you had, I would have booked the next trip to The North Pole to find you."

The clock on the mantle softly chimed twelve times.

"Merry Christmas," Jingle whispered after the last one, and nibbled at her ear lobe.

Bel laughed and her fingers deftly traced the point of one ear. "Merry Christmas, Jingle."

For Bel and Jingle, it was a very merry Christmas and a very good night.

December 25

Christmastown, The North Pole

Christmas Day

Santa Claus gratefully sank into the comfortable overstuffed chair in his private study and pulled the snowglobe toward him. Mrs. Claus set a tray on the table and settled in the other chair.

"How was this year's trip, dear?"

"The best ever!" Santa gave his standard reply as he took the cup of Special Reindeer Milk from his wife. He took a swallow and sighed with satisfaction. She had spiked it with a double shot of rum, just the way he liked it. She usually added peppermint schnapps to hers.

"Any problem with the new reindeer?"

Santa shook his head. "They worked as well with the others as if they'd been doing it for years."

"Splendid!" Then Mrs. Claus peered over her spectacles at him. "Are you sure Alexander is happy?"

"He chose to stay, didn't he? I think the human world will treat him better than the elves ever did."

Mrs. Claus smiled. "I hope so. Alexander had an incredibly difficult time trying to fit in here. Do you think he knows?"

"That he's half human? No, I don't think it ever crossed his mind."

"Perhaps it's best he never finds out." Mrs. Claus set her empty cup on the tray. She looked at Santa, a twinkle in her eye, as she took off her spectacles and removed the pins from her hair.

A cloud of silver-white tumbled to her shoulders and down her back. Santa quickly drained the last of his Special Reindeer Milk. This was his favorite part of their post-Christmas ritual. She stood and took him by the hand, pulling him to his feet. "Are you very tired after your long trip?"

Santa smiled wickedly and tugged on his beard. "Not very. What do you have in mind, my little snowflake?"

"Oh, I think it's time to give you your Christmas present," she said in a low, seductive voice that made him as hard as an icicle. She reached up on tiptoe to kiss him hungrily, tasting sweetly of Special Reindeer Milk and peppermint. Then she took him by the hand and started leading him from the study. "I'm going to give you a night to remember. If you ask nicely...but you have to remember to be naughty."

Santa would remember. After all, night at the North Pole lasted until spring, he thought happily as he followed her to their bedroom.

TWELVE NIGHTS OF CHRISTMAS

Written by

TREVA HARTE

On the 1st Night

Rome Tyler wasn't thinking about much of anything but sex and snow. He was thinking about sex because when you didn't get much, you thought about it a lot. He was thinking about snow because he was getting too much of it all around him.

In fact, he'd cut short his visit with Cindy and Ira so that he could get home before the storm really hit. They'd protested that he hadn't had a chance to really visit, but Rome figured they were just being polite. He wasn't really the social type. He could talk if there was some reason to, but chatting just to chat had never been something he'd been good at.

Christmas wasn't really something he was good at either. He didn't need to celebrate any more today. When he got home he'd start tinkering with some of the graphics he wanted on his next computer game. Maybe he could add the really kick-ass heroine he was mentally toying with at the moment. If he added some of the features he was thinking about, this could become a very adult computer game really fast. Too bad there wasn't as much money in X-rated games.

Rome might have passed by without looking at the usually deserted house located close by the fork in the road he took to his own place. He usually did. But something very strange was going on. Rome squinted though the snowflakes and made sure he was seeing what he thought. Between the storm and early nightfall, he had to check more than once.

A ladder rested halfway down the tree trunk. And it looked like someone in a turquoise snowsuit was dangling on a branch about three feet above the ladder. Someone with – he thought, though he couldn't be sure as he braked and fought to keep the truck steady while it slid to a halt – a very nice butt.

With the truck safely stopped, he climbed out and made his way over to the tree. Yeah. A very nice butt indeed.

Rome picked the ladder up and placed it closer to that butt. He figured he didn't need to ask if the person needed help. People didn't sit out in trees during a blizzard for fun.

"I'm not sure I can get down alone." The voice sounded remarkably calm considering what it was saying. "My legs cramped up a while ago."

Shit. Rome thought about it. He sure wasn't planning to carry someone down a tree, though she looked tiny enough. With an inward sigh, Rome climbed up the ladder. Maybe she just needed some encouragement.

"If I help, can you move?" he asked.

"I'll try."

He didn't like the sound of that, but it would have to do. He twisted the body around, pulled one leg over the tree branch. The woman's face came into view. That was very nice, too. High cheekbones, blue eyes. Pretty. Her hair was covered with a stocking cap so he could imagine what color it was.

"This won't work. My legs don't want to move." Her lips — full and sexy — trembled and firmed again. And then trembled.

God. She was scared and needed help. But he wasn't a fucking superhero. What was he supposed to do? Suppressing a sigh, Rome said, "Can you come closer? I'll try putting you over my shoulders and getting down."

Sure he would.

She shifted her weight and moved toward him and then, somehow, she was settled on his shoulders. He braced himself, took a deep breath and started down the ladder. His hands were sweating inside his gloves.

"I am so sorry." Her voice was husky and whispered right next to his ear. "I saw something up in the tree. It was pink and — well, I've owned birds. I thought it might be some exotic parakeet or something that had somehow escaped and was going to freeze to death. What an idiot."

"What was it?" He forced the words out.

"I told you I'm an idiot, right? Some previous owner must have thrown it up there. I just never noticed it before." He couldn't ask again but she finally went on. "It was a pink flamingo. A plastic pink flamingo stuck up in the damn tree."

He stopped laughing when the wind decided to give a particularly nasty gust. The ladder shook, then swayed. With an inward groan, Rome knew they were toast.

Sometimes it sucked being right all the time. Down they went. Rome saw it all with the clear vision of someone doomed. The ladder was going to go completely to the ground this time, but somehow he managed to keep hold of the woman and a foot on the ladder for most of the way, even though they got banged a time or two against the tree. Then the ladder left his feet entirely. Their fall seemed to accelerate. When he landed on the ground he felt her land on top of him. Well, he'd managed to break her fall at least—

That's when he saw the shooting lights.

On the 2nd Night

"This is ridiculous." Mari felt fine. She didn't even have a cold to show for her stupidity.

Unfortunately, though, her Christmas guest was still asleep. Mari was starting to get very worried. What should she do for him? She understood why it might be hard to get a doctor on Christmas day. But now it was already almost late afternoon on the 26th and still no one but a disinterested receptionist would answer her at Dr. Raines' office. Since the nearest hospital was at least fifty miles away and the snow was packed in solid she didn't think calling anyone there would help.

Checking on the Internet—and the connection had been up and down during the storm—told her that sleepiness could be the sign of a concussion. And if the concussion was mild just rest would help. But what if it was something worse?

Mari stuck her head in again and peeked at the man who was sleeping in her bed. She didn't want to remember how difficult it had been to half-guide, half-drag him there. He wasn't a big guy but he certainly outweighed her.

She didn't even know his name. But he'd hurt himself while helping her. He'd laughed with genuine amusement instead of contempt when she'd confessed why she'd been in a tree during a snowstorm.

After they'd finally gotten inside and she managed to get him close to the bed, he had blinked and in a slurred voice said, "I'm sorry. I think I've gotta pass out now."

He hadn't lied. She had ended up spread-eagled on her own bed, out of breath because his full weight had collapsed on top of her. It had been a little difficult to get either aroused or annoyed when she was wheezing for air. But his body had left...well, an impression on her. And now, with the bedcovers kicked back and his body stretched out all over her bed, she was thinking just how sexy he looked.

Maybe it was because she and Chet hadn't had sex for months before he explained just why he'd refused to be with her. Maybe she was grateful to this guy. After all, he wasn't that good-looking. He'd worn geeky glasses before she took them off. He was thin and only medium height. She liked tall men. His hair was rumpled and badly cut. He definitely needed a shave at this point and she didn't care for men with brown hair. And he was too young for her. She didn't even want to think how young.

Still, she kept looking. And not just to make sure he hadn't died.

Oh God, this was embarrassing. But stripped down to his briefs the way he was, she could see his cock. Or at least she could imagine what it looked like. Mari knew she'd been without one to play with for too long.

But long was the word here. Very long. At least as far as she could tell— and those briefs didn't leave much to imagination.

Mari moved closer to the bed. She ought to check on him and see he was all right. He might have slipped into a coma. He might have gotten pneumonia. He might—

She reached out her hand to touch his forehead. Normal. His eyes opened. His pupils looked all right, not that she was an expert on how they should look.

He had nice eyes, actually. A dark brown almost hidden by long lashes. Then his eyes opened wider.

"Where'd you like to touch me next?" he asked. "My body is at your disposal."

"Where would you like?" Mari heard herself answer.

His smile was slow and really attractive on that severe-looking face. She hadn't teased a man in a long time. Not even verbal teasing. Chet hadn't much liked that and she'd fallen out of the habit.

He opened his mouth and the phone rang. Mari jumped.

"Doctor Raines?" She asked after hearing the hello. Her guest's eyes stayed open and fixed on her face while she talked. "I have a man here who had a bad fall and hit his head."

Mari paused and hissed, "What's your name?"

"Rome." The man shut his eyes for a moment and then added, sounding less certain, "Tyler."

She relayed the name back over the phone and then asked, "What are your symptoms?"

"My head hurts."

She waited. Reluctantly he said, "A lot."

Her guest wasn't much of a conversationalist. Mari wondered if he wasn't very bright or if the fall had contributed to his refusal to say much. Between trying to pry information from her guest — from Rome — and writing down information the doctor gave her, she didn't have time to think about the little interlude they'd had before the call. Much.

Mari finally hung up and sighed.

"So?" he asked.

"So you probably have a concussion, not that I can get you to see the doctor any time soon."

"I hate doctors."

"Perfect. Anyhow. Since there isn't anything we can do to get you out to see the doctor, he says the best thing is to rest, check to see you can think coherently and have no strenuous physical activity for at least a week."

Rome grunted.

Mari decided to test his thought processes.

"How old are you?"

"Twenty three last month."

Wonderful. She'd been peeking at a baby.

"What day is it?"

"The day after Christmas. But since it's getting dark, I'd say it isn't day at all."

"What state are we in?"

"New York. The Adriondacks. And I'm gonna work myself into a state of annoyance if you don't stop with these questions. How old are you? And tell me your name, if we're going to get personal."

"Marigold." Mari heard what she'd said without thinking. "I mean Mari. Everyone calls me Mari."

"Marigold or Mari, which is it? And what's your last name?"

"Edwards. I mean, Adams."

"You sure you haven't been hit on the head?" He almost sounded like he was going to laugh again.

"I was Mari Edwards up until—well, up until two days ago. Now I'm Marigold Adams again, I guess." Mari realized her present conversation could put a healthy man into a coma and tried to get a grip. "I'm recently divorced. My maiden name is Adams."

"How do you do, Marigold?" He reached out to shake her hand. "I won't try to have you answer the age question. That tends to fluster most women and I can see you aren't up to anything too tough."

Great. Now he decided to talk. Smartass. At least his head didn't seem any more addled than most men's.

"How bad is the snow out there?" he asked.

"Well, it's drifted up against the doors high enough so that I can't open them. I suppose I could try to climb out the windows but I'm sure you couldn't."

"No climbing for you." His eyelids began to lower again. "Too dangerous for us both. So..."

She waited but he stopped talking. She wondered if he was asleep again.

His words dragged themselves out at last. "Looks like it's just the two of us here for awhile."

"I have food and warmth. We'll do fine." Unless they got another big storm soon. "I've been working on the house. It's very secure."

"Cozy. We'll be cozy as two turtledoves together. Just you and me." And he fell back to sleep, a half-smile on his face.

Smartass. As least she thought he was being one. But the idea of being that cozy made her bite her lip and fight a sneaking excitement. It was going to be just the two of them for the foreseeable future.

And, oh Lord, he'd fallen asleep with his cock looking pretty damn hard. If he could fall asleep with that, heaven knew what his cock would be like waking up.

On the 3rd Night

He woke up so hard he hurt. He shut his eyes, thinking about the woman in the house with him. The one who was entering his dreams and promising him seduction. Not just seduction, but satisfaction.

Rome let out a soft whoosh of a laugh. Now he was fully awake and he knew what a lie that had to be. He hadn't satisfied a woman in his life. He still remembered the smirk on Lisa's face that evening. He'd spilled himself into her, desperate, aching. She'd been teasing him for weeks. He'd felt about half-crazy.

"Idiot." He whispered aloud.

Why Lisa was around had never occurred to him. Not until the night he'd had too much to drink and she had too few clothes on and...well, there he was. In the middle of humiliation within minutes. He hadn't gotten much satisfaction from that, either.

He needed to keep away from this woman. Somehow. Even though they were trapped in her house together. Even though he could hear her footsteps coming down the hall. Even though he wanted to tumble her into this bed. . .

"Rome? Are you awake now?"

Even though her voice sounded sweet and welcoming.

"Yeah."

"You've been sleeping on and off for almost two days now. If you're awake, you must be starved. Dinner's cooking."

He thought about how starved he was for other things.

"Lemme, wash up a little."

"Can you manage alone?"

"Uh...yeah. Sure." He could manage everything alone, damn it.

* * * * *

Rome eyed the three small birds that Mari was basting. She looked like she knew what she was doing. It smelled good. But he wasn't used to being snowed in with elegance. She had candles for the friggin' dinner table and a tablecloth. And she was fixing something unusual.

"What is that food?" he asked.

"Cornish game hens," Mari said. "I got this recipe from a French chef but don't worry. They'll taste just like chicken, OK?"

Then why not eat chicken? Rome thought about scowling, then decided that hurt too much. The pain was down to a manageable dull throb in the back of his head, but he still felt a little sluggish. He felt like he had a full blown case of cabin fever *and* he felt sluggish.

And he still felt horny. That wasn't helping. Mari had piled her hair up and put on earrings that glinted when she moved. They were probably real diamonds, not rhinestones. She was wearing some kind of silky blue pants and tunic. Who did that out here? Rome tried to decide she was a snobbish snot, but all he could think was how good she looked. Most of the women he saw lately wore jeans and a flannel shirt.

She looked feminine. Elegant, classy and feminine. But she seemed approachable, not snotty. The silk looked touchable. The tunic was cut just low enough that he could glimpse a flash of an ivory bra when she bent over. The bra was almost the color of her skin.

Mari looked up just then and saw him staring. She smiled, a little hesitantly, and he wanted to whimper. That smile did things to him.

He'd managed without any woman for years now. Why the attraction to this one? She did ditzy things then came off looking like an assured member of the elite. She had the strength to manhandle him into her house and then could gracefully light candles placed on delicate crystal candleholders.

He'd spent all day today resting but whenever he came to, he watched her, trying to figure her out. All he'd decided was that she was sexy and he wanted her. He might not get her, but he wanted to.

"What're you doing here?" That question had been driving him crazy all day.

"What?"

"This place was completely deserted until last year when some lawyer bought it for a summer vacation spot. Why are you here now?" He looked around at the freshly painted almost-but-not-quite white walls. "And the house already looks decent. Worked on. Who did the sanding on the floors and put up the new storm windows? No one around the lake was hired to help."

"I was married to that lawyer. He bought the place last year because I begged him to but, more importantly, because one of his managing partners liked the area. Chet thought we could entertain up here and impress people who mattered during the summer." Mari began to toss the salad. "But he didn't care about the place particularly. He was perfectly happy to throw in the cabin to help finalize the divorce."

"And all the work? This place has been an eyesore forever."

"That was me. You see, I'm used to working with my hands. I've had to work on artist lofts before. Real lofts where you had to make something from nothing. I wasn't always a lawyer's wife." She began to grind some fresh pepper into the salad. "I've always been a jewelry designer though. An artist. Artists make beautiful things from what they find. I haven't been able to do everything I want. All I've managed far is the main floor. Upstairs is still frightening."

Mari had sanded the floors, painted the walls, put in windows? She put the salad on the table, turned to the kitchen and began to sprinkle parmesan on the pasta. Damn, she cooked, too.

He watched her walk. She had on an ankle bracelet that clinked just slightly as she walked. She poured wine into what looked like real crystal wineglasses. She must've gotten the glasses in the divorce. Those looked like something a rich lawyer might own.

He felt too young, too uncultured. A barbarian. He had no idea what a woman like this might be interested in.

But he was definitely interested in her. Rome still found it hard to believe what she was saying. Tonight she looked too refined to have sweated over remaking a neglected house into...this.

"You've done all the work here by yourself?"

"Absolutely. I can't afford help. I don't even want help." She put plates on the table. She had to bend over to do it and he got another peek at the bra. "This is the way I want it to be right now. Just me. All alone."

She must be very, very good with her hands. Oh damn. This was a bad time to decide maybe he was in love.

* * * * *

She'd dressed up to impress him. Maybe even intimidate him. To tell herself they were too different. Having him around today had made her crazy. Not impatient crazy the way Chet could make her when he lounged around the house. Rome was making her longing crazy.

It was ridiculous. He hadn't done anything except stare once or twice very intently. He'd been trying to figure her out. That made sense. Of course he would. She was a stranger here. She didn't fit the norm.

Then again, she never did. Chet could never completely transform her into the model lawyer's wife. But she'd learned to look the part. Mari had done her best to look elegant tonight to show Rome how wrong they were for each other.

But Rome hadn't done what she expected — he neither got embarrassed nor dismissed her. He just kept looking. And she kept wanting to look back.

He was making her hands itch to touch. What was it about him?

Oh Lord. She realized that she *was* touching. Somehow she had leaned forward at the table and traced his lips with her finger. So much for elegant hands-off refinement. She'd never been much good at it anyhow.

Rome took her finger and drew it slowly into his mouth. She felt his tongue lick, tentatively. He was still staring, his eyes narrowing on her. Her other hand gripped the table.

This was a mistake. A terrible mistake. Wasn't it? His tongue stroked her finger again, his lips and teeth not letting go. He gave her wet, gentle pressure with his lips. That felt good. Then his teeth were just the tiniest bit rough, promising other delightful things.

Chet would be appalled if he knew who she was fantasizing about. Well, Chet would probably be appalled to hear she was fantasizing at all. He'd expected his wife to behave. She had followed his expectations for years. Maybe that's why he'd turned to a mistress.

To hell with Chet. For just a moment Mari felt the old boldness return. She'd had men before she was married. Interested men. Why wouldn't this man be interested?

Her legs were trembling a little. No. This was too irresponsible. Mari didn't even know this man. And she'd said she wanted to be alone and meant it. She had to be sensible.

Mari felt like she was pulling her hand away from glue, but she managed it. She wasn't sure she'd ever managed to do anything so difficult in her life.

"Sorry." Rome's voice was a little husky. "That was stupid of me."

"You don't have to take the blame. I started it."

He smiled, just a little, before he said, "But it is stupid. The doctor said no strenuous activity for seven days. And what I'm thinking about could be very strenuous."

Mari blinked once. Twice.

"I guess we have a good excuse to just forget these last few minutes then." She couldn't believe the last few minutes had even existed. Of all the bad ideas and wrong people to have those ideas about!

Rome had gone back to staring before he said, "We can forget it, I guess. For now."

On the 4th Night

The phone rang and he jumped. God, he'd finally gotten to sleep after a night of half-waking, half-dreaming hot, unattainable sex dreams. He reached for the telephone groggily.

"Hello?"

"You're still there, eh?" Dr. Raines asked.

Where else would he go? The snow had stopped but it was too cold out for anything much to melt. Mari wasn't able to shovel out and he wasn't up to it.

"Yes." Rome kept it simple.

"Thought you might be in no rush with a pretty lady to stay with. So I got Brad out with the snowplow. Brad's working for a lot of folks but he's willing to get out to Miss Adams' place by the afternoon. I figure after that you can get to my office. I'll expect you before four."

"Yeah. Right. Thanks."

Rome wasn't sure if he really felt thankful or not. But he should be at his own place if he could get there. Of course. Mari was probably sick of bothering with a semi-invalid stranger who couldn't do much around the house to help.

He felt his face. He'd opted not to shave rather than try the ladylike razor Mari offered him. Rome figured he'd break it on the first stroke anyhow. Yeah. Stuck in bed most of the time, no shave, no fresh clothes. Mari would be happy to say good-bye.

* * * * *

Mari struggled out of her dream reluctantly. Warm hands, warmer mouth, hot cock. Unshaven face scraping her face, her breasts, her thighs. The telephone's ring was a rude wakeup.

She heard Rome rustling around in the kitchen. What time was it? She hadn't been able to sleep well last night, thinking about just his mouth and her fingers. Lord knows what she'd do if he'd tried anything serious. Or she had.

She struggled out of bed and belted on her bathrobe. Before she'd even managed to get to the bathroom, the telephone rang again. Mari picked it up this time.

"Hope you had a good Christmas," Chet said. Before she could respond, he went on, "Did you sign those papers?"

"Not yet. I just got them Christmas Eve. They made a great present." Mari remembered other, fancier presents Chet had given her back when he cared about her reaction.

"I'd appreciate it if you expedited the process as much as possible."

"Why the hurry? Is your new woman pregnant?" Mari snapped.

There was a long silence on the other end of the phone.

"I don't think Andrea is relevant to this conversation." Chet had his lawyer voice, the one that gave away as little as possible. But Mari knew.

"Listen, I'm snowed in here. I'll mail the papers back when I can." Mari hung up and prayed Chet would have enough injured dignity not to call back.

She stalked out to the kitchen.

"You want some coffee?" Rome asked and looked at her face. "Umm...a lot of coffee maybe?" He tried a smile but that faded quickly. He was smarter than he looked.

Mari reminded herself that her mood wasn't his fault. Then she looked at the stove.

"My God, what have you done?" she gasped.

"Scrambled eggs."

He looked like he'd fought a flock of chickens for the eggs. She stared at the mess wordlessly.

Rome hid behind a cup of coffee.

Suddenly there was a rhythmic pounding on the door. Mari looked up, startled. That wasn't the wind or snow.

"He's early." Rome stood up. "It's Brad with a snow plow. That means I can get to the doctor and then get myself home. I — well, thank you."

Mari almost yelled *wait*. Then she caught herself. She didn't want him here. She wanted to get out. She was happy that someone had come to rescue them with a snow plow.

"Maybe I can catch a ride with you as far as the post office," she mumbled. Why prolong anything? She ran to her room to grab the papers she had stuffed in her desk just a few days ago. This was as good a time as any to get rid of all the men cluttering up her life.

* * * * *

"I'm glad I could make it in," Mari said. "I'm just amazed any mail made it here at all."

"We're used to snow around here." Barb shrugged. "But I hear there's another biggish storm coming our way soon. You may want to stock up on some supplies again."

The post office and general store, along with the two or three other buildings that made up Pine, were nearby. Mari mentally tried to figure out what she needed that she could carry back easily. This snow could really isolate her. No Rome this time.

And that was fine. She'd get some work done. She might start some work on the upstairs. This was exactly what she'd counted on for this winter.

She swallowed the lump in her throat and prepared to trudge through the cold and snow to the store.

Barb looked at her and gave a sudden wink.

"So what was it like?"

"What?"

"Being with a young buck all alone. "

Barb was easily her mother's age. Mari fought not to blush.

"Fine. He was unconscious most of the time." Mari didn't like the way the smile spread on Barb's face. "In fact, I really didn't get to know him all that well. What does he do for work up here?"

Barb laughed out loud.

"Nothing. He's retired."

Mari laughed, too, then stopped. "Are you serious?"

"Yup. He made a lot of money a year or two ago with computers and decided to quit while he was ahead."

"Hey, Barb!" A man stuck his head in the door. "Phones are down again!"

Barb turned her attention to him. Mari walked out of the post office feeling a bit like she'd been concussed herself. She knew nothing about the man she'd been lusting after.

While she bought groceries, Mari ignored the grins on people's faces. Great. She'd become the topic for gossip before she'd gotten to know anyone. Oh, God. And she'd once wondered if *Rome* was stupid.

She didn't have time to think more as she fought against the rising wind on the way back. The trip was long but uneventful without snow. With snow it was brutal.

Mari pushed her front door open and stared at the living room. It was going to be quiet here. Well, she liked quiet. She had several days' worth of newspapers to read. She had —

As she pulled off her winter coat she began to shiver. She had no heat was what she had. Oh damn it. She was so tired already. And if she could get back to town — would the store or anything be open this late?

She thought of the door to her garage with her truck inside. Of course that was still blocked with huge drifts of snow. Mari groaned.

* * * * *

Brad had been good enough to drop him off at his truck even though there was more plowing to do and more money to be made off it. Of course Rome was paying double for Brad to go ahead and plow through to his place immediately. But it was still nice of Brad. The other man had even helped him clear the mound of snow from Rome's truck before he went on his way.

There was no reason that Rome couldn't just leave now. Except...Rome hesitated, his hand on the door of the truck.

She wouldn't want to see him. She'd hopped out of the snowplow without a second look, with only a quick thank you for Brad. Obviously Rome had taken up enough of her time.

Rome forced the door open, slid inside and started the truck up. Thank God the vehicle worked well in cold. Warmth from the heater began to warm up the cab and melt the remaining ice on the windshield. He could leave in just a few minutes.

Seeing her was crazy. If he did she'd either laugh at him or, if he got lucky and she was glad. . . he'd fail again. Rome hated failure, especially in this case.

He tried to remember all those books he'd frantically read after that fiasco with Lisa and, almost as humiliatingly, after he did as badly with the call girls he'd hired. Books weren't going to help him, Rome had concluded long ago. Besides, even if they could, they were safely stashed away in his house. And he wasn't.

Oh God, he wanted to see Mari. Every stupid cell in his body screamed to see her, even while his brain warned of the disaster that would happen if he did. Desperate, Rome decided on a new plan.

He unzipped his pants and pulled his stiffening cock out. Fiercely he began to squeeze and stroke himself. If he could just take the edge off, he might be able to get through this.

Not that she wanted him, of course. But if he got lucky and she changed her mind, maybe he could manage...Just the images of what he wanted to do to help manage with Mari made him throw his head back and groan.

His release was quick and violent and almost satisfying. Maybe he should try again, just to be safe. Naw.

Walking through the cold to the house ought to be enough. If he had to, he could do that again later.

The idea of having to started to get him hard again. Damn it.

Rome pulled his pants together and then turned off the engine. Taking another deep breath, he slid out into the snow, making his way back to Mari's house.

* * * * *

She couldn't believe she heard a thumping on her door. Someone was here? Thank God. She pulled the door open.

Rome! She let out a quick sob and then bit her lip. How embarrassing.

"Mari? I thought I'd check again because—" Rome sounded hesitant but she'd already thrown her arms around him before her brain registered the hesitancy.

Mari threw her arms around him. "I could kiss you, Rome!"

She saw his startled look but it was too late. All of a sudden he was kissing her instead.

"Oh!" Mari managed before then his tongue was between her lips and dancing against hers. Ohhh.

Maybe it was lucky there wasn't much heat in the house because she was feeling warm. Very warm. Combustible warm. His hands slid up under the heavy woolen sweater she wore, touching skin, and she could feel those fingertips brushing against nerve endings. Nerve endings that were screaming for more of that touch.

Damn it, they were both dressed for cold weather. She couldn't feel *his* skin properly. She nipped his lip just slightly. She was taking over the kiss, wasn't she? Men — well, Chet — didn't always like that. Too late. Her hands had already unzipped his jacket and burrowed inside that flannel shirt.

"Marigold?" His voice spoke against her earlobe.

The use of that name made her pause a moment.

"Marigold, we have to get ourselves out of here. But we can't just leave. If it gets colder your water pipes will break. "

He could think about that right now?

"I turned off the water. But draining the pipes takes forever."

"Not a problem." He took one step slowly back, then another. Finally he turned to the telephone.

"Phones are out." Mari knew her voice sounded breathy.

Rome grunted and pulled out a cell phone from his shirt pocket. Mari tried to compose herself again while he turned his head to talk. He was coming up with excuses to get away from her. She'd scared him with her hunger. She was too old. She wasn't his type. She —

"Hank can come out." His voice cut into her frantic muddle of thought. "He said he'll fix the furnace tonight or at least drain the pipes if he can't. Leave the door open. He'll lock it when he's done."

"What?" Mari wasn't understanding anything.

"C'mon Marigold. You get to stay at my house tonight." He smiled at her. "I can't promise game hens. I run more toward canned chili. But I do have a working furnace — and if not, my house can stay warm with just the fireplaces."

She'd meant to get her fireplaces fixed. Mari scowled defensively. She'd just run out of time and money...Then what he said registered.

"Stay with you?"

"Yup. My turn."

On the 5th Night

His turn. What the hell had made him say that to her? Rome would have kicked himself for stupidity but his cock was throbbing too hard for him to move. He knew damn well why he'd said that. So did his penis.

Mari had looked at him, all wide-eyed and amazed. But she hadn't run. He warned himself she might have agreed because anything was better freezing to death. But she sat close to him in his truck, closer than she needed to.

God, he could smell her perfume. He could feel his hands sweating as he gripped the steering wheel tightly. In a few minutes, less than five minutes, he might be able to get closer to her yet, to touch and taste and smell...

Less than four minutes.

Jesus, Jesus. He might last just about that long inside her if he kept thinking about what they might do together. Rome tried not to hyperventilate.

He was starting to feel a little dizzy between the lingering concussion, lust, fear and his sudden speculation as to how much snow had been dumped on the road in cubic feet—not that his calculations was really taking his mind off what he wanted to do in less than three minutes now. No. Less than two.

He pulled as close to the door as the banked snow would let him and leaped out. Then he went over and pulled the door open for Mari. Yeah. He was gonna show her how gentlemanly he could be.

But not in less than one minute—he opened the door, the living room almost spinning around him.

"Oh, Rome! This is beautiful!" Her face was awed as she looked around.

"I designed it myself—" He didn't want to talk about his house. Rome took one uncertain step toward her. He put his hand on her shoulder and helped her ease her coat off.

He reached out his other hand to touch her breast. Why was it so hard to move his arm? That was when he realized he was pitching forward. Oh damn it. Oh damn it.

He fell forward, both hands outstretched to break his fall.

* * * * *

She was asleep. In the next room. One thin wall away. Rome mentally kicked himself. She'd been that close before. This shouldn't seem different. But he'd been too groggy to fully realize her location before. And it hadn't been in his home. Now he could visualize just how she looked under those burgundy covers of the guest room. He could imagine her curled up in the bed he'd picked for guests. It had an iron headboard. He could imagine her hands gripping the iron rods with her eyes closed as he—

Oh yeah. Rome was wide awake. In disgust, he stood up and walked outside. It must be three in the morning. Since it seemed there wasn't going to be any sex tonight, that left warm milk or cold beer to get him to sleep right now.

And walking. He didn't much feel like walking. But whatever he had to substitute for sleep or sex was going to definitely be second or third best. Walking would do. He stumbled down the hall into the kitchen and stopped.

Sitting next to one of the lights, Mari sat in her bathrobe, her legs curled up on the kitchen chair, putting pencil to paper. She looked up and smiled.

"I know you've overdone today. I hope I didn't disturb you," she said. " I just couldn't sleep."

"I had the same problem." He wondered if it was for the same reason. God, she was pretty, even in that ridiculous robe. The doctor had said Rome seemed healthy enough, but to take it easy for a few more days. If Mari was interested, he'd be willing to risk his health. If he didn't pass out again. If he thought he could do something right for a change with a woman. Oh hell. Those books were still in the study.

Rome scowled as he went to the sink and picked out a mug.

"Warm milk?" he asked. He wasn't going to chug beer in front of Mari this early in the morning.

"That would be nice, thanks. Do you have any?"

She'd probably looked in his refrigerator already. He thought about what he did have stocked up. Milk hadn't been one of the things he'd considered picking up recently.

"Well, I have a box of instant hot chocolate."

Mari nodded. She went back to her writing. Rome started boiling a kettle of hot water, then dragged a chair up from the table. She looked so intent. He shouldn't bother her. He knew how it bugged him to be interrupted when he was designing games –

"What're you doing?" he asked.

"My jewelry designs. Sometimes you just get an idea that you can't forget about. I woke up with some for rings tonight."

Damn. She wasn't thinking about what he'd been thinking. Perversely, he began to wonder how he could make her think about sex. A brilliant idea hit him – so brilliant that he wondered why he'd never thought of it before. Don't Put Your Penis In. It was workable. It was simple. She'd enjoy herself. And eventually he would, too.

"Let me see." He ruthlessly discarded his qualms about intruding. Rome looked over her shoulder, getting close but not crowding.

"Hey!" For just a second he forgot his plans. "Those are good. But can you actually execute that? It looks intricate."

Mari let out a little snort.

"People don't pay me for designs I can't do, Rome. My only problem will be getting this pen-and-ink design to transmit on my computer to some folks who'd be interested. When I lived near the city, I never depended on a computer this much. I could always meet with clients in person." She added a few more swirls to the design.

"I can do that for you," Rome said.

"You could?"

"People do pay me for what I create with computers." Rome looked at her. "Don't tell me you haven't heard something about me in town."

"Just a little. Just today." She smiled again. "I hoped you might offer some expertise."

"Darling, I can offer all kinds of expertise." He stopped talking. Rome knew he was implying more than he could safely promise.

But his body was damn near humming with anticipation. And Mari didn't seem either angry or afraid. This might be the right time. Rome tried breathing through his nose, deeply. Now or never.

"Um...excuse me." He saw Mari staring as he bolted out of the kitchen. But if he could just get his hand on one, just one, of those damn manuals he'd bought he could kick things off with some confidence. And maybe not pass out.

* * * * *

What had she done? Mari stood up and turned the squealing tea kettle off. One minute he had been standing over her, giving her goose bumps with how intent he seemed, and the next he had charged out of the room like she had rabies.

Mari poured the hot chocolate into the mugs and carefully stirred the hot water in. He didn't like people to ask about his work with computers? She still didn't know what he did. She'd been too obvious when she sat there, waiting for him? Mari made a face at her flannel robe. Maybe she hadn't been obvious enough? There was no nightgown underneath her bathrobe but they hadn't gotten far enough for Rome to see that. Now it was too cold to strip down unless she was under the covers with some extra male body warmth. And there was no extra male body warmth in sight.

Mari drank the hot chocolate, lingeringly. She finished the mug and put it down, a bit forcefully, on the kitchen counter. Fine. She'd leave. She wasn't going to bother to clean up after. Let there be sticky hot chocolate around. Let there be dark rings left on the counter. Rome didn't care. To hell with—

"Marigold?" The voice was a little hoarse.

"What?" she asked, not too pleasantly. "Your chocolate is cold."

"But I'm not." Rome walked toward her, his eyes fixed on hers. He put his hands on her shoulders. "Just tell me if I do anything you don't like. Please."

He bent down and began to nuzzle at the V of her robe. The robe parted easily.

"What?" she asked again, stunned.

"Because I want to do everything to you. Anything. Anything you want." She walked backward, wondering if this was another one of her dreams. She'd been dreaming of Rome a lot. He followed her, stopping her flight so that his tongue could flick at her breasts and nipples, his breathing harsh in the quiet kitchen. She let her head fall back for a moment, savoring the pleasure, and then took another step back.

The hard chair that she fell into, making her sit abruptly, felt real.

Rome smiled at her. She thought the smile looked a little strained but didn't have time to think anything more when he got down on his knees before her and pushed the robe even further aside.

Thank God she hadn't worn anything underneath. His tongue was lapping against her thighs, up higher and higher yet. She squirmed. He hadn't even gotten close yet and Mari heard herself let out one little whimper.

He looked up then, startled.

"Is it all right?" he asked.

"Not yet." Mari spread open those lips that were dying for attention. His eyes rested on them as if he couldn't stop. "But if you keep going, it will be."

"OK." That wasn't eloquent but soon he was using his tongue very effectively. He was first tentative, as if to see what she wanted. Mari forgot restraint and pride. She'd been burning up for this man for days. She told him – in whimpers and gestures and sometimes words. Rome soon stopped being tentative.

Yes. His tongue was hot against her cunt and she could feel her wetness mingling with his tongue's. Sensations danced from her clit and twisted up into the rest of her body. When had she last felt this way? It had been so long, too long, she needed…

His teeth tugged a little, making her shudder.

"I need more!" Mari wailed, knowing she was near shattering but not close enough. "Please! Oh, Rome, please come inside!"

He hesitated again, looking up, his eyes dilated almost the way she'd feared they might be when she checked him that first night.

"Oh God! I'm not going to hurt you, am I?" Mari asked, almost incoherently. "I have to feel you, I need you to fill me – "

When had she begged like this? She must have a long time ago, before Chet told her he didn't want a slut but a wife. Rome's finger brushed against her clit while he seemed to ponder whether she'd pleaded enough for her release.

"I want your cock, Rome. In me, stretching me...I can't come until I feel it!" Mari felt herself crying.

"No, Mari. Not yet. But I'll take care of it—" And suddenly something was inside. Not a cock, Mari knew that. But something that stretched her and something hard that rubbed against where she ached most.

She gave up. Whatever Rome wanted, she had to— she moved, and writhed and let whatever the hard thing was do its magic. Mari cried harder as Rome began using friction where she needed it.

Sweat began to trickle down her face. She was wet other places, too. This was so good but not—not quite…

"Your cock, Rome!" She gasped.

"Not…yet!" He was gasping, too.

Why not? And then she was rubbed so expertly that she forgot thought and words and everything as she screamed.

* * * * *

Don't Put Your Penis In was a brilliant fucking plan. The books seemed to agree with it. Except Mari wasn't co-operating. Damn it, Marigold! He wasn't going to get near that beautiful, wet pussy of hers until she came. But she wouldn't.

"Come!" He nearly whimpered it to her.

He used his fingers on her clit, just the way he had when she responded before and he manipulated the spoon with his other hand. She rose half off the chair, shuddering and crying, but he knew she wasn't there yet.

"Please, Mari, come," he muttered again and put his mouth on one tight nipple.

Her head was thrashing from side to side now. She opened her eyes for a half second as if it was almost too much effort.

"Please, Rome?" Her voice was thin and wailing.

The plan. He had to stick to the plan. When her hand unbuttoned his jeans and reached inside though, Rome wondered how anyone could. He was on fire wherever her fingers touched. He could barely see for bloodred pleasure and this time his dizziness wasn't the concussion. Were other men superhuman? How the hell did they hold out long enough?

And then Mari shattered. Oh God. Oh thank you, God. He dropped the spoon and vaguely heard it clatter on the floor as he pulled her onto the kitchen table.

"Oh God," he muttered it out loud as he *finally* freed his cock entirely and oh yes, oh yes, oh yes. He was inside.

Her tight, eager warmth tightened around him in an almost painful but totally pleasurable welcome. She was stretched out on the table looking like his own personal sex slave. This time he'd gotten the idea. Now if he could just last more than four seconds inside her...

"Feels good," he managed to say, even while part of him laughed at his lack of originality.

And then all thought left him as he, too, came.

On the 6th Night

Mari looked out the window to the white world beyond her. Rome's cabin was beautiful. Light-filled, new, filled with little gadgets that she knew he must love. It wasn't like her old, quirky, half-done home but it was equally enchanting.

It wasn't exactly a substitute for him, though. Mari rubbed her arms to fight a chill that had nothing to do with the warmth Rome's heating system provided.

What had she done?

Well, what she had done was have a shattering climax last night. And then Rome had joined her and had his own. Everything had seemed perfect.

Then he'd pulled out, looking absolutely horrified, and said, "I'm sorry."

She hadn't seen him since.

He was somewhere in his study, she imagined. She could hear movements in there and the hum of a computer. The cabin was big but not so big he could lose himself entirely. Still, since it was obvious he didn't want to be seen, Mari wasn't going to force herself on him — the way she had before? Was that what had happened? She had no idea.

Mari sat down to doodle in her sketch book. Work wasn't very appealing right now but it was that or go absolutely crazy guessing and second-guessing what had gone wrong. And then she became absorbed in her design.

* * * * *

"Mari?"

She looked up, blinking.

"Rome?" She felt the pleasure before she felt the sting of embarrassment. But when the shame arrived, it hurt even more because she's forgotten about it for…hours?

"Aren't you hungry?" His voice was hesitant.

"Well, I guess." Mari focused back on the kitchen and saw the clock on the wall. "It's that late?"

She hadn't gotten anything out for a meal. Of course it was well past supper. Mari had a vague feeling she'd skipped lunch, too.

"I'm sorry. I should've prepared something." Chet had always been furious when she forgot to cook dinner.

"I'm the host. I guess I should've." He moved slowly into the room, as if ready to scuttle out again at the first sign of trouble. "So what would you like? I cook canned soup, chili or spaghetti."

Mari opened her mouth to offer to prepare something and shut it again. No. She wasn't going to push for anything from him.

"I'm hungry." She hoped that wouldn't be misconstrued. "Anything is fine."

"It's late. I guess soup is quickest." Rome wasn't looking at her as he moved to the kitchen cabinets. Mari kept her mouth shut. Whatever the problem was, it was still there. Rome poured the can's contents into a pan. She heard him swallow before he turned. "Mari, I am sorry."

"Why?" She was proud she sounded so calm.

"I'm not—" He swallowed again. "I'm a lousy lay. I'm sorry."

She gaped.

"How long did I last? Two seconds? That's even shorter than my previous record and, believe me, that was hard to beat." His voice dripped self-contempt as he turned to stir the soup.

"You—Rome—"Mari forgot everything she was about to say. "You aren't using *that* spoon, are you?"

She rushed forward to snatch the...Their hands touched as she looked down.

"Oh. It's a ladle." Mari felt a hot blush starting. "I just— Rome, you were unhappy about your performance last night?"

"Yeah."

That was what was wrong? That's what had given her a nervous stomach all day?

"You stupid goose!" She snapped the words out. Mari saw his face and realized how he'd taken that. "No, wait!"

She got him a split second before he took flight. Her hand grabbed his upper arm, hard.

"What?"

"I didn't mean it that way. I meant you had nothing to worry over. I enjoyed myself." She saw how stunned he looked and smiled. "Sleep with me, Rome?"

On the 7th Night

Now she knew he was in his study. The door was locked—she'd finally been desperate enough to check. Mari hadn't stooped to pleading with him outside the door, but she was coming close.

Maddening man. For a smart man he could certainly misunderstand her. When they woke up this morning she'd meant for them to have fun. Instead he ran away.

Mari went back to work, but she had no concentration. She caught herself sketching erotic scenes in her sketchpad. And thinking about Rome.

She found herself eating a very late dinner alone and worrying over how hungry he must be. Mari would've shaken herself if she could once she realized that. She'd just gotten rid of one unreasonable man.

Maybe a hot shower would make her stop worrying.

* * * * *

She wouldn't let him touch. Rome tried not to sulk as he sprawled in the hot tub, his eyes shut. He would have sulked more if she hadn't done what she did this morning.

They'd slept together. Just sleeping at first. That had been new. Rome found he liked feeling a woman against him at night. Very much.

Maybe too much. The first time he woke up hard late at night, he'd eased himself away and masturbated. Mari was sleeping and he didn't want to be any more of a...a goose than she already thought he was. And she was sleeping so soundly.

The second time he woke up hard Rome tried to remember what the damned manuals had suggested. An early morning hard-on when a woman was next to you was hell on the nerves and memory.

He didn't think he'd made too much noise but Mari's eyes had opened. She smiled. Then she got on all fours and began to suck that hard cock.

"Keep your hands to yourself, Rome," was all she said. He did. His clenched fists damn near broke the headboard posts, but he did.

She might not have used words but her little gasps of appreciation and the way she slurped up his cock was more than eloquent. Rome told himself it wasn't his fault he'd bucked and moaned and shuddered and come – once again fast – under that mouth and tongue.

When she sat back, he saw her nipples were hard. His hand reached for her but she rocked back, laughing.

"Oh no. I'm going to get my payback later." She touched her own nipples and then her clit. Rome felt himself starting to harden again.

"Mari?"

"Later, Rome. You can't touch—me or *you*—for the rest of the day." And she slid her finger from her pussy and raised it to his lips.

Oh God. He could taste her and smell her and — Then she took the finger away.

"Later."

He'd avoided her after that. Until later. But how much later was what he wanted to know. When he started walking doubled over in pain? The hot tub was the only thing that was keeping him from complete agony.

He heard the splash of another body entering the water. Without saying hello, Rome slid underneath the surface of the bubbling water while he decided what to do about that damnably tempting female body.

On the 8th Night

He was beautiful in a way she hadn't really seen before. But she hadn't seen him completely naked, his body sleek and subtly muscled, like a runner's. He looked at her with drops of water in his eyelashes and his eyes laughing and glittering.

Mari bit her lip. He was beautiful and young and she wasn't.

What was he thinking of when he saw her?

Rome had emerged from the hot tub, laughing. Then his breath caught. She was so beautiful. She sat with her breasts half submerged under the water, little wavelets rippling around her. Rome couldn't figure out what she was thinking as she looked at him, a small smile on her mouth.

She didn't laugh much but even her smile was attractive, enticing. Sensual.

God, he wished he knew how to impress her. She'd probably had men who knew their way around a woman's body. Men who could make women moan and beg for more. He thought of her moaning and begging for someone else and his gut tightened. Then he thought of her moaning and begging for him and something else tightened.

He didn't know what to do. But he had to try.

"Mari?"

She opened her arms. They met and slid underwater together. The water's current pushed at them and, nudging her forward, Rome pulled her legs apart to let the bubbles flow between her legs. He slid behind her, his cock resting against her rear, his legs curling over hers to anchor them in place, his hand shielding and guiding the underwater spray so it would tickle, not hurt.

They stayed under as long as they could and then both surfaced again, Mari laughing the way he had before.

"That was sooo outrageous, Rome!" She turned so her slick body rubbed itself against his. "And I'm so glad you have a hot tub."

"Happy New Year, Mari. A little late. It's just past midnight." He'd forgotten until now but being with her had started making him think of a new year that might contain the two of them...if he could just manage —

He carried her to the bench attached to the tub. OK. Don't Put Your Penis In, with variations. When he wasn't working on the cyber-Marigold he'd been studying his books. He could do this.

"You look tense." Mari didn't look tense at all. She twined herself around him. "We have to work on that."

"How?"

"I can think of a few ideas. How well do you follow directions?"

"I didn't touch you all day, did I?"

"You thought about me. Constantly." Her smile showed she wasn't complaining.

"All I did was think...fantasize."

"I know. Me, too."

"That does *not* calm me down."

"I don't want you calm, Rome."

"That's fine. I think I've figured out some more."

"Rome—"

But Rome, absorbed in what he was looking at, bent his head down. He was almost sure he could do this.

Until Mari leaned forward and licked his cheek.

"You look so delicious with those drops of water right there," she told him.

Oh *God*. Desperately, Rome lowered his head and began to torment his tormentor. From the taste, just the taste, of Mari on her finger earlier he'd remembered he loved pussy. Mari's, anyhow. And there it was, just out of the water, waiting to be tasted.

* * * * *

She was going to drown. If not from the water as she tilted her head back, then from the sensations. Had she ever had anyone concentrate on her body the way Rome was right now? Had she ever seen anyone with a face tense with his own desire to carefully make sure she was satisfied? Never. If she had she'd still be with whoever it was—and probably flat on her back the way she was now, urging him on.

The wavelets slapped at her body, beating out an irregular rhythm as Rome's tongue traced an erotic path against her clitoris. Mari could feel her hips moving, her whole body drumming as Rome worked his way thoroughly up and down, side to side. The water and his tongue combined were driving her out of her mind.

She felt the tension coiling, spreading, and his mouth inciting more.

When she broke, falling into a pleasure that made her cry, she could hear his noisy breath even as she moaned.

"Now you." Mari managed. "What do *you* want?"

Anything. For pleasure like that, anything. Besides she wanted his cock now. She'd take it with her mouth or hard up inside her. She wanted to milk him of everything he had, to make him groan and grow limp from pleasure the way he had for her.

Rome said nothing and she remembered her role.

"Get on your knees and straddle me," she said.

"What?" He looked barely able to concentrate. She understood.

"Now, Rome."

And he obeyed. This way she could see his cock, thick, demanding. Well, she was about to demand, too.

"Masturbate."

He looked down, hesitated, then, suddenly, he threw his head up, eyes shut, and began to stroke that cock. Mari wanted to whimper. She could feel him shaking above her.

"Stop. You can touch any part of your body but your cock or your balls now."

"My God, Mari!" His voice was thick. "You'll kill me."

"Not yet." Mari resisted reaching out to finger the length of cock in front of her. "Not just yet. You're going to learn something."

And then she watched, squirming herself, as his hands hesitantly stroked at the insides of his thighs, close but not touching the forbidden areas. And then one hand began to fondle a male nipple, making it turn into a tight, hard point.

His breath grew harsher yet. He was sweating. Mari shivered. She was making him do this. *Her.*

Mari couldn't stand it. Her hands reached up to cup his balls. So tight.

"Mari, no—" Rome sounded agonized.

And then his hands were on his cock, squeezing. She could feel him spill out, on top of her, moist and hot.

There was a long silence.

"Rome—" She'd pushed too quickly.

He shook his head, rejecting her words. Rome just let his hands trace up her legs, past her thighs, and then, without saying anything else, he swung himself out of the hot tub and away.

On the 9th Night

Things were not going well. They knew why. Rome didn't lock himself away now. Not physically. But everything about him as he stalked through the house said *don't get near me*.

Rome spent a long time outside, chopping wood. Mari peeked outside, watching him—admiring him. There was strength there and grace and…what did it matter anyhow? He was avoiding her.

Why wouldn't he have sex with her? No matter how bad it was, it couldn't be this bad. And why wouldn't the idiot just listen to her? She wasn't any sex expert but she had some ideas.

"Stupid man." She put the lunch dishes in the dishwasher. She'd eaten alone again. He was going to starve.

"I suppose I am."

Mari jumped at the voice behind her. There he was. Rumpled, unhappy, but no longer dancing away from her. Rome was very solidly there.

"Let me fix a sandwich." Mari could have kicked herself. Why was she acting like a wife?

He opened his mouth. She knew he wanted to refuse but his stomach began to growl. Loudly. He said, less than graciously, "Sure. Thanks."

She made him his sandwich and plunked it in front of him.

"Listen, Rome, if you won't come near me, maybe I should go. The weather has cleared up some. I bet my furnace is working again."

"Probably. Fine. If you want." Rome didn't look at her as he began to wolf down the sandwich. "I cleared out enough that we can get to your house."

He wasn't supposed to say that! Mari gulped.

"Fine."

If that was the way he wanted it, fine. Mari could do her own avoidance dance. He could freeze before she'd see him again this winter. His balls could fall off. He could—

"I'll be ready in ten minutes," Mari said.

On the 10th Night

He missed her.

His cock missed her pussy, but even worse, he craved Mari. He wanted to see Marigold at the kitchen table, drawing her designs or fixing him food, or just—just being there. He'd already gotten used to having her body in bed with him. One night with her and he woke up wondering why she wasn't there.

Damn it. He'd been on his own for a long time now. He'd thought he did fine being alone. Better than with someone. Alone you could work as late as you wanted, eat when you wanted and think what you wanted.

Of course he had with Mari, too. But it was better with her.

"I don't know what to do." He admitted it out loud.

Boy genius admits defeat. He'd go and ask Mari to come back—to take him in. Anything. But what good would that do her? He'd kicked her out. Apparently things weren't going to get better with his sex life. If he was going to spend his life sexually frustrated, wasn't it better not to inflict his moods on someone else?

Mari would find someone who could do things in bed he couldn't—

"Fuck that." Rome said out loud.

He looked at the clock. Wonderful. Almost midnight again. He couldn't get her now. Couldn't even call.

He heard the knock and leaped for the door.

"Rome?"

Her voice was like music. Timid music, maybe but music.

"Why are you here?" Damn, he hadn't meant it that way.

Mari's smile almost reached her eyes.

"Your hot tub."

And she began to strip on her way toward it.

On the 11th Night

She was in the hot tub before he reached her, looking at him wordlessly.

Rome began to strip too. Maybe he was asleep. Maybe this was a fantasy. No, the water felt real.

"You came for my hot tub?"

"Sort of. You weren't coming for me so I came after you." Mari looked at him. "I came back so you'd listen to me. The way you should've when I asked the last time we were here. You didn't. You insisted on doing things your way."

"Damn it, how else can I—" He shut his eyes. "What do you want me to do?"

Her ideas couldn't be any worse than the ones he'd tried so far.

"Well, the first one is simple, really. Whenever you feel ready to come, stop moving."

"What?"

"You're a bright guy. You figure it out. It's not that difficult."

Rome thought about half a second. To try her suggestion out he could take her to bed or—he slid her against the side of the hot tub and then he slid himself into her. They knelt, eye to eye.

Rome breathed through his nose. He wasn't moving. Unless you counted the trembling that was starting in his legs. This was too much. He wasn't going to make it. He—

"Think about something else." Mari sounded a little breathless herself.

Oh God. What?

"What have you been working on recently?" Mari asked, as if they were having a normal conversation. As if her muscles weren't gradually tightening around his cock.

The hot tub was turning into a cauldron. And Mari might well be a witch.

"My new software game." Rome thought about saying things coherently. He could do this. He knew how to focus his mind on things even when there were outside distractions. Like Mari's legs bumping against his hips in the water.

"Tell me about it."

"I have a new heroine. Her name is Marigold." He grinned. "She's hard to pin down. Very sneaky. Very...slippery." He risked a stroke down Mari's wet back. "But she has formidable opponents."

"A mad computer scientist type, perhaps?" Mari asked.

"That would work." Rome could visualize that. "He really is mad. About her."

He could feel some control coming back. Enough so that he risked a little stroking inside Mari's pussy. That felt good. Good but he was all right. Yeah. Rome's hand slid down, caressing, trying for the right spot between her thighs.

"Ohhhhh!" He must've found it. Mari twisted against him.

Her eyes shut. Yeah. He was watching her come apart and he was still...safe.

"Rome, you're a devil—" Mari opened her eyes again. He liked making her eyes dazed.

"You wanna know my full name, Marigold?" He almost felt like there were two Romes. One that was moaning inside him begging for release, the other watching Mari lose control and reveling in his own power. So far the powerful one was the winner.

"What?" She leaned forward and her breasts bobbed against his chest. He breathed through his nose again. He was going to make her climax with him in her. Still hard.

"Stephen Jerome Tyler. Junior."

"Oh!" Mari stared at him. "I know you! I mean, I've actually read about you in *Newsweek*."

"That was a lousy photograph of me. I had a beard." He ventured a thrust this time. Yes.

"Rome, you're famous." Mari leaned her forehead against his shoulder and nibbled his earlobe. "Oh, forgot. I didn't mean to try to stimulate you. This time."

"It's OK." Rome wanted to laugh—or maybe beat his chest. Mari knew him. She finally knew who he was and she was more concerned about having him continue his...his sex lesson.

So was he. His hand stroked that responsive clit of hers again and she bucked against him. Yes. And then he bent his head and sucked on her nipple. Yes. Feeling her shuddering was almost better than feeling his own excitement.

Not that it wasn't starting to creep in despite his best efforts. Maybe that would be OK. Maybe. But not yet.

"Mari?" Her head was nuzzled against his neck and shoulder. He could feel her breath coming faster. Even though it killed him, he pulled himself out. Too dangerous. "I'm — getting damn close again. Help."

Her hand reached out to touch the tip of his penis. And then she squeezed. Hard.

"*Damn* it, Mari!"

She looked up. A little annoyed but still mindful of his goal he went back to his hand's touching, circling movements. The sensual dance he could make this lady do. Even if she did try to injure him.

"Sorry. But that keeps your mind off..." She began to say. He thrust in hard. He felt her fingers claw into his back. Her heels began to drum against him. And then her face contorted and he could feel her begin to climax.

Yes! Fireworks, victory dance, twenty one gun salute, tidal wave...it was all that and then some. Rome could finally move hard and harder yet. This was bliss. This was paradise. This was...he lost track of vocabulary and screamed wordlessly himself as Mari began to ruthlessly milk him of every last drop of his semen, making her own high piping cries of excitement. This was how it was supposed to be. He'd done it. He was the Lord of Creation, the Emperor of Sex.

And, once again, he came inside Mari.

On the 12th Night

"Mmmmm?" Mari murmured, sleepily. They'd made it to bed last night, somehow. Rome hadn't been sure he could ever get hard again afterwards, but he was starting to realize he was more resilient than he thought.

"Even when we're not snowed in...I'd be happy to have you stick around."

"What does that mean?" Mari sounded more awake.

"You and me. I'd like that." Rome knew that wasn't the most romantic proposition but that wasn't his specialty. His heart drummed in his chest while he waited for her to answer.

Mari seemed to understand though she looked hesitant. "Rome. I'm not very good at the sticking around part."

Rome thought about that. "Mari?"

"What, Rome?"

"You know what they're forecasting?"

"More se—I mean, more snow?"

"Several more days of it. And nights."

"You'll kill me with sex, won't you?" Her hand reached out to stroke his hardening penis as she leaned over him.

"I'll try," Rome said, modestly. He'd read men lasted longer with women on top. He was quite willing to give that a try. There was probably still more if he ever had time to get back to those manuals. "Besides, that gives me some time to change your mind. And, of course, pick up a few more…pointers."

On the 1st day of Christmas my true love gave to me...

A Partridge in a Pear Tree

On the 2nd day of Christmas my true love gave to me...

Two Turtle Doves

On the 3rd day of Christmas my true love gave to me...

Three French Hens

On the 4th day of Christmas my true love gave to me...

Four Calling Birds

On the 5th day of Christmas my true love gave to me...

Five Gold Rings

On the 6th day of Christmas my true love gave to me...

Six Geese A-laying

Twelve Nights of Christmas

On the 7th day of Christmas my true love gave to me...

Seven Swans A-swimming

On the 8th day of Christmas my true love gave to me...

Eight Maids A-milking

On the 9th day of Christmas my true love gave to me...

Nine Ladies Dancing

On the 10th day of Christmas my true love gave to me...

Ten Lords A-leaping

On the 11th day of Christmas my true love gave to me...

Eleven Pipers Piping

On the 12th day of Christmas my true love gave to me...

Twelve Drummers Drumming

SANTA CLAWS

A Wyndham Werewolf Story

Written by

MARYJANICE DAVIDSON

For Giselle McKenzie.
If not for her, this would have been a very different story.

Chapter One

Alec Kilcurt, laird of Kilcurt Holding and the most powerful werewolf in Europe, stomped through the snow and slush and wished he were anywhere, anywhere but here.

He stopped and stood obediently with the rest of the herd, waiting for the light to change. Snow was spitting down on him with malice he could almost feel. It did nothing for his mood. He disliked leaving his home for any reason, but being called to America to pay homage to The Wonderful Child was a bit much.

And now he was shamed; his duty had never seemed a chore before. He admired and respected the pack leaders, Michael and Jeannie Wyndham. Michael was a good man and a fine leader; his wife was a crack shot cutie and baby Lara was adorable. Since the cooing, drooling infant was likely to be his next pack leader, Alec's presence — the presence of every country's werewolf head — had been required for both political and practical reasons. The pack was some 300,000 werewolves strong; unity was both a desire and a necessity.

Unfortunately, visiting the Wyndhams in their happy home just exacerbated his own loneliness. He'd been searching for a mate for years, but had...how did the humans put it? Never found the right girl. He thought it was funny that human women complained their men didn't commit. An unattached werewolf male was likely to want to move in after the first date. What was a man, after all, without a mate, without cubs?

Nothing, that's what. Meeting baby Lara was a great relief; pack leaders without heirs made everyone nervous. Seeing Michael's happiness, on the other hand, was a torture.

Now his duty was done, and thank God. His plane left Boston tonight, and nothing was keeping him from it.

Faugh! More snow! And not likely to be much better, even when he got home. Really, there was nothing to look forward to until spring. Others of his kind might enjoy romping through the slush on all fours, but here was one furry laird who hated getting his feet wet.

And Boston! Grey, drizzly, dreary Boston, which smelled like damp wool and exhaust. He felt like pulling his scarf over his nose to muffle the smells of

(peaches, ripe peaches)

unwashed masses and

(peaches)

He stopped suddenly, and felt a one-two punch as the couple walking behind him slammed into his back. He barely felt it. Hardly heard their complaints. He spun, pushed past them. Walked back, nostrils flaring, trying to catch that elusive

jangleJANGLEjangleJANGLEjangle

intoxicating

jangleJANGLEjangleJANGLEjangle

utterly wonderful scent.

He stiffened, not unlike a dog on point. There. The street corner. Red suit trimmed with white. White gloved hand shaking that annoying bell. Belly shaking like a bowlful of jelly. The glorious smell was coming from Santa Claus.

jangleJANGLEjangleJANGLEjangle

He charged across the street without looking, ignoring the blaring horns, the shriek of airbrakes. The closer he got, the better Santa smelled.

JangleJANGLEjan—

"Jeez, there's no rush," Santa said in a startled contralto, pulling down her beard to squint up at him. Her eyes were the color of Godiva milk chocolate. Her cheeks were blooded, kissed by the wind. Her nose was snub. Adorable. He felt like kissing it. "I mean, the bucket and I aren't going anywhere."

"Nuh," he said, or something like it.

"You really should forget that whole 'pedestrians have the right of way' attitude when you're in this town...errr...everything okay?"

He had been looming over her, drinking her in. Now he jerked back. "Fine, everything's fine. Have dinner with me."

"It's ten o'clock in the morning." She blinked up at him. A stray snowflake spiraled down, landed on her nose. Melted.

"Then lunch."

The woman looked down at herself, as if making sure that, yes, she was dressed in the least flattering outfit a woman could wear. "Are you feeling okay?" she asked at last.

"Never better." It was the truth. This was rapidly turning into the best day ever. He had visions of spending the rest of the day rolling around on Egyptian cotton sheets with Santa. "Lunch."

She peered at him with adorable suspicion. "Is that a question? Is this your first day out of the institution?"

Right, right, she was human. Be polite. "Lunch. Please. Now."

She burst out laughing, putting a hand on her large belly to keep from falling into the street. As if he'd let that happen. "I'm sorry," she gasped, "but the absurdity of this...you...and...it just hit me all at once." She cut her gaze away from his to smile at the woman who had just tucked a dollar into her bucket. "Merry Christmas, ma'am, and thank you."

Now that he was no longer gazing into her eyes, he felt much colder and realized his feet were wet. Faugh!

"I can't have lunch now," she said kindly, looking back at him. "I can't leave my spot until noon."

"Not even if you made lots of money before then?"

"Not even if the *real* Santa came along to relieve me."

"Noon, then."

"Well. All right." She smiled up at him with timid liking. "You'll be sorry. Wait until you see me out of this Santa outfit." The spasm of lust nearly toppled him into the gutter. "I'm not at all cute," she finished with charming idiocy.

"Noon," he said again, then pulled his roll from his coat pocket. He plucked the money clip off the wad, and dropped the eight thousand dollars or so into her bucket. "I'll be back."

"If that was Monopoly money," she hollered after him, "lunch is *off!*"

Chapter Two

Giselle Smith watched the visitor from the planet Hunk stride away. When he'd rushed up to her, she had nearly dropped her bell. There she was, jangling for charity, and then Hunk Man was *right there*. She couldn't believe the speed at which he'd moved.

His hair was a deep, true auburn. His eyes were a funny kind of brown, so light they were nearly gold. His nose was a blade and his mouth—oooh, his mouth! A girl could stare at it and think...oh, all sorts of things. He was tall, too; she had to crane her neck to look at him. Over six feet, for sure. Shoulders like a swimmer. Knee-length black wool coat, probably worth a grand at least. Black gloves covering big hands; the guy looked like he could palm a basketball, no problem.

He had come charging across the street to, of all things, ask her to lunch. And to give her thousands—thousands!—of dollars.

Her, Giselle Smith. Boring brown hair, dirt-colored eyes. Too short, and definitely too heavy. The most interesting thing about her was her name. Which people always got wrong anyway.

Obviously a serial killer, she thought sadly. Well, we'll have lunch in a public place where I can scream my head off if he starts sharpening his knives.

It was too bad. He was really something. What the hell could a guy like that want from a nobody like her?

* * * * *

Alec watched the woman (he was still angry at himself for not getting her name...or giving his, for that matter) from halfway down the block. His spot was excellent: he could see her perfectly and, better, he was downwind.

He thought about their conversation and cursed himself again. He'd babbled like a moron, ordered her to lunch, stared at her like she was Little Red Riding Hood. Yes, like Little Red...hmmmmm.

He wrenched his mind from that delectable mental image

(the better to eat you with, my dear. eat you all...up!)

and concentrated on thinking about what an idiot he had been. It was a miracle the woman had said yes. It was a miracle she hadn't hit him over the head with her bell. He had to be very careful at lunch; it was imperative she not spook. He thanked God he was weeks away from his Change; if he'd caught her scent any closer to the full moon, he'd have scared the pants off her. Literally.

God, she was so *adorable*, look at her, shaking her little bell for all she was worth. Many people stopped (pulled in, no doubt, by her allure) and threw money in her bucket. As they should! They should give her gold bullion, they should lay roses at her feet, they —

He pushed away from the wall, appalled; someone hadn't put money in! An expensively dressed man in his late thirties had used the bucket to make change, and went on his merry way.

Alec got moving. In no time he had closed the distance and flanked the man, had snaked out a hand and pulled him into a handy alley.

"Wha-aaaggh!"

"This is cashmere," Alec said, his hand fisting in the man's coat.

"Let go of me," the man squeaked, reeking of stale piss — the smell of fear. "Or I'll yell rape!"

"Your shoes," Alec continued, undaunted, "are from Gerbard in London, and didna cost you less than eight hundred pounds." Only Samuel Gerbard used that kind of supple leather when making his footwear; the smell was distinctive. "And that's a Coach briefcase."

"Gggglllkkkk!"

Perhaps he was holding the man a little too firmly. Alec released his grip. "The point is, you c'n stand to share a little this holiday season."

"Wha?"

"Go back," he growled, "and put money. In. The bucket."

He let go. The man fled. In the right direction — toward his Santa sweetie.

A minute later, Alec was back at his post. He checked his watch for the thirtieth time in the last half hour. Ninety minutes to go. An eternity.

An eternity later, at 11:57, he realized the skulking teenagers were ready to make their move. The three of them had been casing the block for the last fifteen minutes, had been watching his lunch date much too closely. It was the bucket, of course; they wanted lunch money...or the eight grand he'd dropped in. It would be laughable, except one of them smelled like gun oil, which meant he had to take some care.

Their path took them right past him; he reached out and slammed the one with the gun into the side of the building. The boy—a child in his late teens—flopped bonelessly to the sidewalk.

His friends were a little slow to catch on; they finally turned when they nearly tripped over their unconscious leader. And saw Alec, standing over the unconscious punk, smiling. Well, showing them all his teeth, anyway. "Take somebody else's bucket," he said. Oh, wait, that was the wrong message entirely. "Don't take anybody's bucket," he called after them, but it was too late, they were running away.

He looked at his watch again. It was noon!

Chapter Three

"It's Giselle," she said to Hunka Hunka Burnin' Love. "Giselle Smith. And you're...?"

"Alec Kilcurt. You have a lovely name."

"Yeah, thanks. About that. The never-ending compliments. What is your deal? Now that I'm out of costume, you can see I'm nothing special."

He laughed at her.

She frowned, but continued. "Too short, too heavy —"

He laughed harder.

" —but you keep complimenting me and I'm waiting for the other shoe to drop. You're a census taker, right? A salesman? You want to sell me a fridge. A timeshare. A kidney. Stop laughing!"

He finally sobered up, although the occasional snort escaped. He snapped his fingers, and the glorious redhead at the next table, who'd been studying him while pretending to powder her nose, gave him her full attention. Her eyelashes fluttered. She licked her red, glistening lips.

Alec held out his hand, and after a puzzled moment the redhead placed her compact in his palm.

"Obliged," he said carelessly. Then he snapped it open, showed it to Giselle. "This is what my people call a mirror," he said in his ultra-cool Scottish brogue. "Y'should spend more time looking in one."

"I know what a mirror is, you goob," she snapped. "Too damn well. Stop shaking that thing at me or you won't get anything nice for Christmas." She nudged the bag at her foot; it held her costume. "I've got friends in high places."

"Are you getting angry with me?" he asked, delighted. He handed the compact back to the redhead with barely a glance.

"Yes, a little. You don't have to look so happy about it."

"Sorry. It's just...I'm a lot bigger than you are."

"And almost as smart," she said brightly.

"Most women find me a little intimidating." He smiled at her. Giselle felt her stomach tighten, then roll over lazily. God, what a grin. "In my...family...we treasure women who speak their minds."

"Then you've won the lottery today, pal. And you never answered my question. What are you up to?"

He reached out, and his big hand closed over her small, cold one. His thumb burrowed into her palm, stroked it. Her stomach did another slow roll, one she felt distinctly lower. "Why, I'm seducing you, of course," he murmured.

Multiple internal alarms went off. "Who *are* you?" she said, almost gasped.

"No one special. Just a lord looking for his lady."

"Oh, you've got a title, too? Well, of course you do. That's the way this day is going."

"It's Laird Kilcurt."

"But your name is Kilcurt. Isn't your title supposed to be completely different? Like Alec Kilcurt, laird of Toll House? Or something?"

He laughed. "Something. But my family does things a little differently. Too bad…I like the idea of being laird of chocolate chips."

The waiter came, refreshed their drinks, and put down the two dozen oysters she'd ordered. She pulled her hand away, not without major reluctance. Since she figured this was her first and last date with the man, she'd ordered recklessly. He'd probably flip out when the bill came. Probably spent all his money on clothes and, given his trim waistline, only ate porridge once a day.

Wrong again. He nodded approvingly at the ridiculous size of her appetizer. He was leaning back in his chair, studying her. He had, if it was possible, gotten even better looking since morning. The expensive coat was off, revealing a splendid build showcased to perfection in a dark gray suit. His brogue, she noticed, came and went, depending on the topic of conversation.

"You haven't lived in Scotland your entire life," she observed, sucking down her second daiquiri. Normally not a big drinker, she felt the need for booze today.

"No. My family often had business on Cape Cod, so I spent a lot of time in Massachusetts. And I went to Harvard for graduate school. I've probably lived in America as many years as I've lived in Scotland."

Titled, gorgeous, rich, smart. Was she on Candid Camera, or what? "That makes sense…I noticed your accent comes and goes. I mean, sometimes it's really faint, and sometimes it's pretty heavy."

"It's heavy," he replied, "when I'm tired. Or angry. Or…excited."

"Okay, that's *it*," she said, slamming her glass down. "Who *are* you? What do you want with me? I made

$18,000 last year. I'm poor, plain, cursed with child-bearing hips — and ass — and I'm prospect-less. What the hell are you doing with me?"

His eyes went narrow. "I'll have to find the people who convinced you of such things. And have a long chat with them."

"Answer the question, Groundskeeper Willie, or I'm out of here."

He looked puzzled at her pop culture reference, but shrugged and answered easily enough. "I'm planning to spend the day getting you into my bed. And I'm thinking about marrying you. *That's* what I'm doing with you, my charming little chocolate treat."

She felt her mouth pop open. Felt her face get red. If this was a joke, it was a pretty mean one. If he was serious, he was out of his fucking mind. She seized on the one thing she could safely question. "Chocolate treat?"

"Your eyes are the color of really good chocolate...Godiva milk, I think. And your hair looks like fudge sauce. Rich and dark. It contrasts nicely with your pale, pale skin. Your rosy cheeks are the...cherry on top."

She downed the rest of her drink in two monster gulps.

Chapter Four

"I'm sorry," she groaned. Sweaty strands of hair were clinging limply to her face and temples.

"It's all right, lass."

"I'm so sorry."

"Don't fret. I've been puked on before."

She groaned again, this time in complete humiliation. She hadn't thrown up near him. Hadn't thrown up around him. Had actually barfed *on* him. On *him*!

"You promised to kill me," she reminded him hoarsely. The elevator doors slid open and he scooped her easily into his arms, and carried her down the hallway. "Don't forget."

His chest rumbled as he choked down a laugh. "Now, I didna promise to kill you, sweetheart. Just to take you up to my room so you c'n get your strength back."

"I'll be all right once I get off my feet," she lied. Death was coming for her! She could feel its icy grip on the back of her neck. Or was that the ice from her third — fourth? — daiquiri? "Just need to get off my feet," she said again.

"Sweetie, you're off them."

"Oh, shut up, what do you know?" she said crossly, getting more and more dizzy as the ceiling tiles raced by. "And slow down. And kill me!"

"Usually ladies wait until the second date before begging me for death," he said, straight-faced. He paused outside a door, shifted his weight, and somehow managed to produce the card key, unlock the door, and sweep her inside without putting her down.

Two hotel maids and a woman in a red business suit were waiting for them. Giselle had a vague memory of the woman in red examining her while the sound of running water went on and on in the next room. She kept fuzzing...that was the only way to describe it. One moment things would be crystal-clear—too sharp, too loud—and the next she could barely hear them for their mumbling. It was annoying, and she told them so. Repeatedly.

" —lukewarm bath make all the difference—"

" —just got so sick, it's verra worrisome—"

" —mild food poisoning—"

" —she'll be okay in no—"

" —close to your Change for it to be a problem?"

" —canceled my flight earlier, so she can—"

" —push fluids—"

She reached up blindly. What's-his-name

(Alec? Alex?)

caught her hand, held it tightly. "What is it, sweetie? D'you want something to drink?"

"No, I want you to STOP YELLING! How can I quietly expire if you keep screaming?"

"We'll try t'keep it down."

"An' don't humor me, either," she mumbled. "Oh, now, what's this happy crappy?" Because now she was being undressed and helped off the bed. "Look, stop this! Isn't there an ice bucket or a hammer or something in here? All you have to do is hit me in the head *really hard* and my problems will be over."

"You'll feel better in twenty-four hours!" the woman in red screamed.

"Jesus, do I have to get out the hand puppets so you people understand? Not so loud! And I'll be dead, *dead* in twenty-four hours, thank you very much, and—where are we going?"

The bathroom. Specifically, the bathtub. She started to protest that a change of temperature in her state would kill her, but the lukewarm water felt so blissful she stopped in mid-squawk.

And that was all. For a very long time.

* * * * *

Giselle woke up and knew two things at once: 1) she would burst if she didn't get to a bathroom within seconds, and 2) she was ravenous.

She stumbled through the darkness into the bathroom, availed herself of the facilities for what felt like half a day, and brushed her teeth with the new tooth brush she found on the counter.

While she swished and gargled and spat, the day's humiliating events came back to her. Working the bell, meeting Alec, being wined and dined—and God, he'd been *flirting* with her!—then throwing up on him (groan) and the table tipping away from her.

Everything after that was, as they say, a blur. Mercifully so. She wondered where Alec was. She wondered where *she* was.

She stepped back into the hotel room—Alec's hotel room—and stole to the window. She saw an astonishing view of the New England Aquarium and, beyond that,

Boston harbor. It was very late; after midnight, but well before dawn; the sky was utterly black but there was little traffic moving.

So she was on the wharf, then. Probably the Longwharf Marriott. She'd often wondered, walking by, what it would be like to stay there with someone glorious.

Well, now she knew.

She turned to look for the light and saw Alec for the first time. He was sitting in the chair by the door, watching her. His eyes gleamed at her from the near dark.

She screamed and would have fallen out the window if it had been open. As it was, she rapped her head a good one on the glass.

"Yes, a typical date in nearly every respect," he said by way of greeting.

"And a good evening to you, too, dammit!"

"Morning, actually."

"You scared the *crap* out of me." When she'd first seen him—it was a trick of the light, obviously—but his eyes had—well, had seemed to gleam in the dark, the way a cat's did at night. Very off-putting, to say the least. "Your eyes, Jesus!"

"The better to see you with, my dear. And it's Alec."

"Very funny." She leaned against the radiator, panting from the adrenaline rush. "Never do that again."

"Sorry." He swallowed a chuckle. "I was watching you sleep. When you got up and made such a determined beeline to the bathroom, I was afraid to do anything that might slow you down. Were you sick again, sweetie?"

"Uh, no. And about this afternoon—"

"When you—er—gifted me with your daiquiris and oysters and swordfish and hash browns and *tarte tatin*?"

"Let's never speak of it again," she said determinedly.

He laughed, delighted, stood in such an abrupt movement if she'd blinked she'd have missed it, and crossed the room. In another moment he was holding her hands. "I'm so glad t'see you're better," he said with such obvious sincerity she smiled—for the first time in hours, it seemed. "I was worried." Except in his charming brogue, it came out *sae glad tae see yerrr betterrrrrr. Ai wooz worred.*

"I'm pretty damned glad to be feeling better myself. God, I've never been so sick! I guess I'd be a terrible alcoholic," she confessed.

"It wasna the alcohol. The doctor said it was food poisoning. I'fact this hotel is full…quite a few guests of the restaurant suffered from the oysters and are resting up because of it."

She thought she ought to pull her hands out of his grip, but couldn't bring herself to take the step. His hands around hers were warm—almost hot—and looking up into his unbelievable face was just too good right now. "What doctor? Was she the lady in the red dress? I remember someone in red who wouldn't stop with the shrieking…"

Alec's lips quirked in a smile. "Dr. Madison is a verra soft spoken woman, actually. You were just sensitive to noise while you were sick. I called her when you—uh—"

"Remember. We're not speaking of it."

"—became indisposed," he finished delicately, but he wouldn't quit smiling. "She helped me take care of you."

"Oh." Touched, she squeezed his hands. "Thanks, Alec. I guess I was a lucky girl to be out with you."

"Lucky?" The smile dropped away. "It was my fault you got sick, so the least I could —"

"Your fault? Held me down and shoveled in the oysters, did you?" she said dryly. "Hardly. In case you haven't noticed the inordinate size of my ass, I'm a girl with a healthy appetite. I got so incredibly sick because I ate so incredibly much."

He squeezed her fingers in response. She had a sudden sense of crushing power held in check. "I adore your ass." *Ai adorrrre yuir arse.* Was she crazy, or was his brogue getting thicker by the second? What had he said? That it came out when he was angry or...

Or...

She snatched her hands out of his grip. "Paws off, monkey boy. Time for me to get the hell out of here."

"I'd prefer it if you didn't call me that," he said, mildly enough. "It's quite an insult where I come from."

"They've got a real mad-on against monkeys in Scotland, eh? Whatever. Gotta go now, it's been fun, buh-bye."

"Can't go." He folded his arms across his chest and smirked at her. "Your clothes were quite ruined in the incident-that-shall-ne'er-be-named."

For the first time, she realized she was wearing a flannel nightgown. It had a demure lace collar which scratched her chin, and the hem fell about three inches past her toes. How could she not have noticed this before? She'd just used the bathroom, for God's sake. Sure, she'd had to pee so bad nothing else had registered, but...she made a quick grab and found she was wearing her old panties beneath the gown. Whew!

His eyebrows arched while she groped herself, but he wisely said nothing. "The doctor said you needed rest and quiet until you — er — purged your — "

"Oh, Christ."

"Anyway." He turned brisk. "I had the staff send up something for you to sleep in."

Any thoughts he was embarked on sinister seduction fled as she fingered the gray flannel. She felt like an extra on The Little House on the Prairie. "Thanks." She smiled in spite of herself. "Flannel?"

He shrugged. "It's cold where I come from. I wanted you to be comfortable."

"And I am," she assured him with a straight face. "But I would be more comfortable if I got the hell out of a stranger's hotel room."

"Stranger?" He grinned at her, all devil and mischief. "After all we've been through today? Shame!"

She laughed; she couldn't help it. Quick as thought, his hand came up and caught one of her curls; he pulled it and watched it spring back. Uck. "Sorry."

"Don't, now."

"No, really...I know, I look like Bozo the Clown on mescaline. If Bozo didn't have red hair. And was really short. And was a woman. You should see it in the summer...giant fuzzball! Hide your children!"

He was eyeballing her hair. "I'd like to see it in the summer."

"Okey-dokey," she said, humoring him, "and *I* would love to see my uniform. I can wear my Santa suit on the subway home."

"At two o'clock in the morning? Alone?" He sounded mortally offended. "I think not. Besides..." His voice became sly. "Aren't you hungry?"

Hungry! Oh, God, no one in the history of Santa bellin' for bucks had ever been this hungry. She actually swayed on her feet at the thought of eating.

"That's my girl. Let's call room service. Anything you want."

"I'll have to get my wallet—"

He frowned forbiddingly. "Do not get your wallet."

"Fine, we'll fight about it later. Where's the menu? God, I could eat a *cow*."

"I know the feeling."

She ordered a steak *au jus*, rare, with mashed potatoes and gravy and broccoli and half a loaf of wild rice bread. "This is going to be really expensive," she warned him. "Are you sure I can't...?"

"Quite sure. It's such a relief to be with a woman who eats." He sat beside her on the bed and sighed. "I'll never understand the American custom of starvation. You're the richest country in the world and the women don't eat."

"Hey, not guilty. As you can see by the size of my ass."

"Tempting. Let's see how well you do with your dinner first."

She glanced uncertainly at him, caught his low-lidded look. It seemed incredible, but the man was actually turned on at the thought of her non-toned ass. His words hadn't been enough to convince her, but his thickening brogue was telling.

It was all very strange. Not to mention marvelous. And oh-so-slightly alarming.

Chapter Five

She did very well. Polished it all off, then ordered ice cream. He watched in pure delight. And thanked God again he was nowhere near his Change.

Keeping his hands—and mouth!—to himself was beginning to be a sore task. It hadn't been a problem when she'd been so miserably ill, but she was obviously feeling better...he could hardly talk to her; his tongue felt thick in his mouth. She was just so—just so adorable, alive and sexy and fragrant. When he'd tugged on one of her glossy curls, it had taken nearly everything he had to keep from plunging both hands in her hair and taking her mouth.

He'd been wild with worry for her, hadn't left her side for a moment since she threw up her lunch on his shoes. He was going to see that chef's head on a pike—or his name on a termination slip—before the sun set again.

"That's better," she sighed, patting her mouth with a napkin. It was a lovely mouth; wide-lipped and generous. When she smiled, the upper lip formed a sorceress's bow. He had to concentrate very hard on *not* sucking that lip into his mouth. "Now. About my imminent departure. Not that you haven't been a perfect gentleman. Because you have. Yes, indeedy! But, bottom line, I haven't known you for twenty hours." She stood and began pacing. "So I'm definitely not sleeping in your hotel room. Anymore, I mean."

"S'don't sleep," he teased, catching her hand and pulling her toward him. Her dark gaze caught him, held him. A line appeared between her eyebrows as she frowned. He kissed the line.

"Now listen here, Grabby McGee...ah!"

He kissed the sweet slope of her neck. And was lost. He might not have been, had she not instinctively leaned into the caress of his mouth. He reached up, found the soft splendor of her hair, and caught her mouth with his. She smelled like surprise and vanilla bean ice cream.

"Oh, God," she said, almost groaned, into his mouth. "You're like a dream. The best dream I ever had."

"I was thinking the same thing."

"What? I'm sorry, your accent—" She giggled and kissed his chin. "It's so thick I can barely understand you. Which, by the way, I'll take as a compliment to my own massive sexiness."

"Y'should. Stay with me."

"I can't." She was wriggling—regretfully, but still wriggling—out of his grasp. Trying, anyway. He had no trouble whatsoever keeping her in the circle of his arms. "I'm sorry. I'd love to. I can't. Leggo."

"But you must." He found her breast—not easy, given its encasement in sensible gray flannel—and cupped it in his palm. The firm, warm weight made his head swim. "You're for me and I'm for you, lovely Giselle. Besides, I'm not going to let you leave."

"*What?*"

"Besides, what if you heave?"

"Oh. I thought—look, I feel fine. I don't think I'll be sick again."

"But what if y'are? I promised Dr. Madison I'd look after you for the next twenty-four hours. It's only been about six."

"But I feel fine."

"But I promised."

"Well...if you promised...and if it's doctor's orders..." She was weakening. She wanted to be persuaded. So he'd persuade her, by God.

Chapter Six

One minute they were having a (reasonably) civilized conversation, and the next his hands were everywhere. Her nightclothes were tugged, pulled, and finally torn off her. His weight bore her back on the bed.

"Alec!" Surprise made her voice squeakier than usual. "For crying out loud, I feel like I'm caught in an exercise machine—yeek!" 'Yeek' because his head was suddenly, shockingly between her breasts, his long fingers were circling one of her nipples, then tugging impatiently on the bud. Heat shot through her stomach like a comet. And speaking of comets, what the hell was *that* pressing against her leg?

"I don't think this is what the doctor had in mind—" she began again.

"Giselle, my own, my sweet, I would do nearly anything you asked." He was having this conversation with her cleavage. "But will you please stop talking for just a minute?"

"Forget it. I reserve the right to chat if you've reserved the right to rip up my nice new nightgown," she informed the top of his head. And her old panties. Well, at least it wasn't laundry day. No Granny underpants on her, thank you very much!

She was striving to sound coolly logical, matter-of-fact, but his mouth was busy nibbling and kissing and licking; it was too damned wonderful. Distracting! She meant distracting. She ought to kick him in the 'nads. Why *wasn't* she kicking him in the 'nads? Or at least screaming for help?

Because he wouldn't hurt her. Because he wanted her with a clear, hungry passion no man had ever shown her. Because she had a crush on him the size of Australia. Because if she screamed he might stop.

"Uh...help?" she said weakly, a moment before he rose up and his mouth was on hers. He smelled clean and masculine; his lips were warm and firm and insistent. His tongue traced her lower lip, then thrust into her mouth. Claimed it. His groin was pressing against hers and she could feel his...er...pulse.

She tore her mouth from his, not without serious regret. If he kissed her like *that* again, it was all over. Good-bye, good-girl rep. Hello, new life as a slut puppy. "Condoms!" she shouted into his startled face. "I'll bet you a hundred bucks you don't have any."

"Of course I don't," he said indignantly. He was— ack!—shrugging out of his shirt. His chest was tanned (in December!) and lightly furred with black hair. She actually moved to see if his chest hair was as crisp as it looked, then pulled her hands back and clenched them into fists. "I didna come here to mate. Have sex, I mean. I'm here on business. I never thought—"

"Yeah, well, that's a problem, Buckaroo Banzai, because I didn't exactly line my bra with prophylactics, either. Which means looky but no nooky. In fact," she added on a mutter, "we shouldn't even looky."

"But you're on the Pill—ow, dammit!"

She'd formed a fist and smacked him between the eyes. The only way he would have known she was taking birth control pills is if he had gone through her purse while she was sick; she'd stopped at the pharmacy on the way to work and picked up her prescription.

"We had to," he said, as if reading her mind. He rubbed the red spot on his forehead, which was rapidly fading. "Dr. Madison was concerned we'd have to take you to the hospital. She needed to know if you were taking any medication."

"A likely story," she grumbled, but it sounded plausible, so she didn't follow up with a headbutt. Not that she'd ever done one in her life, but how hard could it be? "And it's the Minipill, Mr. Knows-So-Much. Besides, I'm not worried about getting pregnant—"

"You should be," he teased. Except she doubted he was really teasing.

"I'm worried about catching something. Without condoms our options are—thank God—limited. Saran Wrap and a rubber band? Forget it. For all I know you could be crawling with disease. I could be taking my life in my hands if I let you bone me!"

"*Bone* you? Crawling—" He got up off her—weep!— and started to pace. Shirtless, and with an interesting bulge beneath his belt buckle. She struggled to keep her gaze on his face. Well, his shoulders, at least. "First of all, my family—we don't—that is to say, I've never been sick a day in my life, and no one I know has ever had—er— problems in that area. Second, I know for a fact *you're* disease-free."

"How?" she asked curiously. He was right, of course, but how'd he know?

"It's hard to—never mind. And third...third..." He laughed unwillingly and ran a hand through his hair. It stuck up in all directions but, instead of looking silly, it only made him look immensely likeable. Adorably rumpled. "Giselle, you're unlike any woman I've ever known. You—" He shook his head. "There's just something about you. I can't put it into words. Come back to Scotland with me."

She'd been busily arranging the covers over herself, though it was a bit late for modesty, and looked up. "What? Scotland? You mean, like a visit?"

"...sure. A visit." He grinned. "Starting tomorrow, and ending never."

"Yeah, yeah. Look, if you still feel like this tomorrow...later today, I mean...I could leave you my phone number." *And never hear from you again, most likely.*

"We need Santas in Scotland," he said seriously. "It can be a verra lonesome place."

"Oh, come on!" She started to get the giggles, and laughed harder when he pounced on her like a big cat. A good trick, since he'd been standing several feet away from the bed. The man was in great shape, no doubt about it. "Now, cut it out...get off, now! I told you, no condoms, no nooky."

"What if I could prove I wasn't—er—how did you put it? Crawling with disease?"

"Prove it how?" she asked suspiciously. Part of her couldn't believe they were having this discussion. The last time she'd had sex had been...uh...what year was it? Anyway, the point was, this was *so* unlike her.

Well, why not? Why not jump without looking for once in her ridiculously dull life? The most interesting thing about her was her name...Mama Smith had been Jane Smith, of all the rotten jokes, and wanted her kid to be remembered. It didn't work. Short, plump women with brown hair and brown eyes weren't exactly noticed on the street.

Until today.

"Okay," she said slowly, "and back off a minute, let me think." She pinched his nipple, hard. He yelped and reared back. "That's better. Okay, if you can prove you're disease-free, I'll stay the night with you." She forced herself to meet his gaze. Her face was so red she was sure her head was going to explode, like that poor schmuck in *Scanners*. "I'll do anything you want until the sun comes up. You've got my word on it. And a Smith never goes back on her word. This Smith, anyway," she finished in a mutter.

He looked at her, wide-eyed. Then turned so quickly—snake-quick, it was uncanny—and grabbed for the telephone.

"Wait a minute, who are you calling?" she asked, alarmed. She hadn't thought he could prove a damn thing at two o'clock in the morning. "If it's some buddy in Scotland who's gonna back you up—"

"I'm calling Massachusetts General Hospital," he said, grinning widely. "Good enough? Dr. Madison has staff privileges there. She's been looking after my family for years and years. She'll tell you all about my medical history if you like."

He put the phone on speaker, so she could hear the hospital operator. Madison was paged, and soon came to the phone.

"How are you feeling, dear?" she asked. She also had an accent, this one the clipped intonation of a blue blood Bostonian. "I had a terrible time calming Alec down while you were ill."

"I'm — ack!"

"No idle chit-chat," Alec said in her ear, and ran a finger all the way down her spine.

She turned and slapped his hand away, then grabbed for the receiver so Alec wouldn't hear the rest of the conversation. "I'm fine, much better...listen, does Alec have any STDs that I, as a potential — ack! — sexual partner should know about?"

"STDs? You mean like AIDS or — oh dear — "

Giselle held the phone away, the better not to be deafened by the woman's shriek of laughter. A few seconds later, Doc Madison had it under control: "Sorry about that. I give you my word as a physician and a lady, Alec has never been sick a day in his life. Nor any of his family. They're a...a healthy lot." Another chuckle. "Why do I have the feeling I'll be seeing more of you, dear?"

"Beats the hell out of me. Okay, then, tha — " That was as far as she got before Alec was tossing the phone across the room, and her back on the bed.

Chapter Seven

"Ah..."

"Don't be afraid."

"I think this is an excellent time to be afraid. For one thing, a) you're a lot bigger than I am, and b) I'm pretty sure you'll tackle me before I get to the door."

"A) you're right, and b) you're right. You're welcome t'try, though." His eyes gleamed. "I like to play Chase."

Oh, Jesus. She slid from the bed and he was right behind her. "Now, now," he said, almost purred, "a promise is a promise. Right, Giselle sweetie?"

Odd, the way he said that...like it was one word: Gisellesweetie. She liked it. Liked him. And a good thing, too, since they were about to get down to it. "You're right. I gave my wormmmphhh!" His mouth was on hers, he was pulling her toward him and she went up on her tiptoes. His tongue was in her mouth, jabbing and darting, and she could actually *feel* that between her legs. One of his hands was on the back of her neck, holding her firmly to him. The other arm was around her waist—luckily he had long arms.

He broke the kiss. With difficulty, she was delighted to see. As for herself, she was panting as if she'd just run a marathon. And as elated as if she'd just won one. "Now," he said, almost gasped. "You said anything. That you'd do anything. Until the sun came up."

"Yes." It was hard to breathe. Black excitement swamped her. A promise *was* a promise, dammit, and she had his personal physician's word that he wasn't sick. More, she trusted him implicitly. She had been handed a fantasy on a plate, and meant to take full advantage. After tonight she'd never see him again. But by God, she had tonight. "Yes, anything. Anything you want."

"Ooooh, verra good," he crooned, almost growled. He sank to the bed and pulled her down with him. And kept pushing her down until she was on her knees, facing him. "Unbuckle my belt. Please," he added with a wolfish grin.

She did, with fingers that were clumsy and stupid. She finally pulled the belt free and wordlessly handed it to him. He tossed it in a corner. "Since you're keeping your promise — so far — we likely won't be needing *that*." She gulped — what the *hell* had she gotten herself into? "Now. My slacks, love. All the way off."

She did so, and then, when asked, relieved him of his boxers. It was too dark in the room to see their color — navy blue? puce? — but by their slippery feel she guessed they were made of silk. No flannel for *him*.

"Now," he breathed. "Kiss me."

She understood him perfectly, and kissed the head of his cock, then rubbed her cheek against him like a cat. He smelled warm and musky and undeniably male. He was also quite thick; she had difficulty closing her fingers around him. "Again," he groaned, "kiss me again, Giselle sweetie."

She did so, tasting the saltiness of pre-come. She licked it off, then licked up and down the length of him. She could feel his bristly pubic hairs tickling her chin on the down stroke. His hand came up, caught a handful of her curls, fisted. "Now," he growled, "open your mouth. Wide." His voice was so gritty she could hardly understand him, but it didn't take a rocket scientist to understand what he wanted—needed. Then he was filling her mouth, her throat. He withdrew in time for her to take a breath, then was in her mouth again. His hips were pistoning toward her face and she realized he was *fucking* her *mouth*. While part of her was wildly excited, her practical side reminded her that although she could count the number of blow jobs she had given on one hand, she was definitely *not* a swallower.

His other hand had found her breasts and he was kneading, squeezing. The sensation of his hands on her, his cock in her mouth, was as exciting as it was overwhelming. She tried to pull back but his grip tightened, and then she felt him start to throb. Shockingly, suddenly, her mouth was flooded with musky saltiness and she reared back, but he had a grip like iron. In a second he had pulled free of her but clapped a hand over her mouth. "Swallow," he murmured in her ear. "All of it. Right down." *Aoull oof it. Ret daeown.*

She did. "Bastard!" she cried, making a fist and smacking him on the thigh. "A little warning next time, all right?"

"I promise," he said solemnly. "The next time I'm about to come in your mouth, I'll give ye ample warning. Ouch!"

"I've never done that before."

He was rubbing his thigh where she'd pinched him, hard. "I could tell."

Incredibly, pierced vanity was now warring with outraged propriety. "Well, *hell*, I'm not exactly known as Slut Girl around here, and besides, I didn't exactly plan—"

He stopped her with a kiss. "You were wonderful," he said warmly. He nuzzled her nose for a moment. "And I'm verra sorry if I startled ye. But I needed ye t'do that for me. Now I can touch you wi' a clear head. Now the fun can *really* start."

"You're still a bastard," she said sulkily. She could still taste him in her mouth, her throat. "You didn't have to make me—"

His smile flashed in the dark. "Well enough. But now it's y'turn, sweetie."

Her irritation lessened as he eased her back on the bed and knelt between her legs, disappeared entirely as she realized he was going to be as good as his word.

It seemed as though he spent hours between her thighs: kissing, nibbling, sucking, and licking, ah, God, the licking. Lots of it, slow and steady; the man never got tired. In no time her clit was enthusiastically throbbing, and that's when he started paying special, extended, loving attention to the little button Giselle hardly thought of unless she was enjoying the evening with Mr. Shaky.

His tongue darted and stroked; she could feel its warm, wet length sliding and slipping between her throbbing lips. Felt him sucking on her clit with a single-minded enthusiasm that was as exciting as it was astonishing.

After a while she was squirming all over the bed, trying to get away from the delectable torture of his mouth. He wouldn't—he—he never stopped, never got tired, just kept at her, at her, at her. Lick lick lick and suck suck suck and even small, tender bites. She could feel herself getting drenched and would have blushed if she hadn't been so close to shrieking. She'd start to feel her orgasm approach, and he'd somehow know, and back off. Instead of giving her the last few flicks of his tongue to push her over the brink, he'd move to her inner labia and gently suck them until she was no longer close to coming, or his tongue would delve inside her — so deeply! — leaving her clit bereft.

"Oh, *God*, y'smell so damned good!" After that breathless declaration he buried his face between her legs and commenced tormenting her anew. His hands spread her thighs so wide her knees were almost parallel, baring her fleshy mound for his hungry mouth. He started licking her in long, slow, agonizing slurps, from bottom to top, over and over and over. Her back bowed and she was certain she was about to lose her mind if she didn't come *now*.

So she squirmed and wriggled, and when she made progress getting away from him he simply grasped her thighs and pulled her back to his mouth. This went on for about seventeen years, until he tired of playing with her, sucked her clit into his mouth, and slipped two fingers inside her. The feeling of his warm lips on her, his long fingers in her, was exquisite, mind-boggling. His fingers moved, stroked, pushed hard inside her, pressure that was just short of discomfort, pressure that was amazing, mind-boggling. His lips had closed over her clit while his tongue flicked back and forth with dizzying rapidity. Her orgasm crashed over her like a wave and she shrieked at the ceiling.

When he came up to lie beside her, she was still shaking. "Better?"

"Oh my *God*. Do you have a license to do that? You ought to be against the law." She reached out and did what she had longed to do an hour ago: gently stroked his chest hair, then followed a path down to his groin. She found him thick, hard, and ready for her. He sucked in breath when she gently closed her fingers around him. "By the way," she added cheerfully, if breathlessly, "I'm on to you. There's no way you're an ordinary guy. Not that I mind."

He stiffened, though whether it was from what she had said, or what her fingers were doing, she couldn't tell. She was squeezing and releasing, squeezing and releasing. Her other hand slipped lower until she was cradling his testicles in her palm, testing their warm weight. "You've got a butterfly's touch, Giselle sweetie," he said, almost groaned.

She almost giggled; she'd never pictured her plump self as something so light and delicate as a butterfly. Alec was no doubt mumbling nonsense because all the blood had left his head some time ago, and gone significantly southward.

She slipped her hand up, down, up, down, with excruciating slowness, with all the care he had shown her a few moments ago. She wasn't terribly experienced, but she *was* well read. She'd been buying Emma Holly's books for years. "That's why you shouldn't mess with a bookworm," she whispered in Alec's ear. "We know some pretty good stuff." He didn't answer her, but because she had brought her palm across his slippery tip and circled, circled, circled while her other hand stroked, she didn't expect him to.

She had meant to keep playing with him as long as she could draw it out, but he suddenly jerked away from her and kneed her thighs apart. He was terse, silent, but oh, how his hands were shaking. "Shouldn't you buy me dinner first? Again, I mea—eeeeeEEEEEEEEEEE!" He entered her with one brutal thrust, all the way, all at once. She was slick, more than ready for him, but it was startling — a little frightening, even — all the same.

He started to drive himself into her.

She squirmed beneath him, felt her eyes roll back in her head...ah, Jesus, this was almost too much! Almost. "Alec."

His hips were shoving against hers, his eyes were tightly closed; his mouth was a narrow line.

"Alec."

"Sorry," he muttered. "M'sorry. Wait. I'll be — nice again. In a minute."

"Alec."

"I can't — stop. Just yet. S-Sorry. So sorry." His hands were on her shoulders, pinning her down, keeping her in place for him. His sex was rearing between her legs, into her, out of her. Digging, shoving, filling her.

"Alec. If you do it a little faster, I'll be able to come again."

That got his attention; his eyes opened wide. And then he smiled, a grin of pure male satisfaction. And obliged. She heard the headboard start slamming against the wall and didn't give a tin shit. She wriggled for a moment until he let go of her shoulders, then brought her arms around him and her legs up. And started doing a little pumping of her own. Their bellies clapped together, a lustful, urgent beat.

His eyes rolled back: "Ah, *Jesus!*" His mouth found hers and he kissed her savagely, biting her mouth, her lips. Then he abruptly pulled back, as if aware he was nearing a line he wasn't ready to cross with her — absurd, given what they were engaged in. His head dropped and she could feel his face pressing against the hollow between her neck and shoulder. There was a sharp pain as he bit her.

He's marking me, she thought. She heard a purring tear as he tore the sheets. *He's making me his own.* That thought—so complicated, so strange, and so completely marvelous—spun her into orgasm.

He stiffened over her as she cried out; his grip tightened—painful for a split second, then he relaxed. "Do that again," he growled in her ear, then bit her earlobe.

"I can't," she gasped, almost groaned. And still he was busy, still he was fucking her with long, fast strokes.

"Yes."

"I—can't!" Pump, pump, pump, and her neck stung where he had bitten her. As if sensing her thought, he bent to her and licked the bite, then kissed her mouth.

"I need to feel your sweet little cave tightening around me again," he said into her mouth. "I must insist."

"I'm done, please, I can't anymore, please, Alec—" Oh, but her body was betraying her, she was arching her back so as to better meet his thrusts, and she could feel that now-familiar tightening between her thighs, the feeling that told her she *would* do it again, thank you very much. "Alec, please stop, please, I can't. Stop! St—" Then it was singing through her, *tearing* through her, and this one made the other two seem like mild tickling in comparison, this one was the biggest thing to ever happen to her.

She felt him stiffen above her again, but, oh, Christ, he wasn't done, he was still thrusting. He seized her knees and pushed them wide, spreading her, making her wider for him. She screamed in pleasure and despair: more of this was sure to kill her. It'd be the best death ever, but it'd still be death.

"More," he muttered in her ear.

"...can't."

"Can. Will."

She reached down, stroked his ass, felt, groped...then shoved her finger inside him, right up his ass, as far as she could. At the same time she clenched around him

(thank you, Kegel exercise)

and was gratified to hear his hoarse shout. Then he was pulsing inside her and throwing his head back and roaring at the ceiling. The headboard gave one more loud THUMP!, and was quiet.

She sobbed for breath and he soothed her with gentle strokes and small kisses. "Shhhh, sweetie, you're all right. I just don't think *I* am. Shhhh."

"That was — that — "

"Easy. Shush, now. Get your breath back."

As the ripples from her last, titanic orgasm faded, she realized she still throbbing. Still wanted him. She was a bookworm cursed with the body of a slut.

"That was — mmbelievable. 'Mazing." Oh, great, she was babbling like a cheerleader after her fifth beer. She tried again. "Unbelievable. Amazing. I'm sure you hear this all the time, but that was the best *ever*. I don't mean for me. I mean in the history of lovemaking."

He was kissing her forehead, her mouth, her cheeks. "For me, also. And I don't hear it all the time. I haven't been with a lady in almost a year."

She nearly fell off the bed. "What? *Why*? You're so — I mean, the overall package is just — and then what you can do in the bedroom—what the hell have you been waiting for? Did you lose a bet?"

"I did not. Who," he said. "Who the hell have I been waiting for. That's the question." He bent and nuzzled her cleavage. "God, I could get lost in you. So easily. Which means I have to kill you or marry you."

"Har, har. And get your nose out of there, it tickles." She could feel his cock on her thigh, very warm, and reached out. "Jesus! You're hard again!"

"Sorry," he said dryly. "I can't much help it if you've got the sweetest cunt. Not to mention some *very* talented fingers."

"No, I mean...uh. I don't know what I mean." Their gaze met. Her eyes had long ago adjusted to the dark; she could see him quite well. "Do you want to keep going?"

He smiled slowly; it was like an extra spoonful of sugar being stirred into really good coffee. "Do you?"

"That's not really relevant," she said tartly. His eyebrows arched. "A promise is a promise, remember?"

"What I like about you—one of the things—is that you're not done. With me." His hand slid down the soft mound of her belly, cupped her between her legs. Then he gently parted her, and his fingers slid up inside her. She sucked in breath and moved with his hand. "You haven't closed off," he murmured into her mouth, "the way a lady will when she's had enough." She could hear herself whimpering softly as his fingers slid in and out and around, as he got slick with their juices. "Of course, you have other qualities, very fine ones." His voice held a teasing note. "But I wouldn't have guessed at this one while I was wooing you over lunch."

"Wooing me?" she gasped. "Is that what you were doing?"

"What I was *doing* was concentrating on not bending you over the nearest table and taking you until my knees gave out. I'm amazed I was able to talk to you at all — ah, God, that's sweet, Giselle. Those sounds you make in the back of your throat make me forget everything. Come down here."

He pulled her until she was kneeling before the bed. She could feel him behind her, holding her around the waist, then stroking her buttocks and kneading the plump flush. "I could bite you here about a hundred times," he muttered.

"Better not if you want to save room for breakfast." She yelped as his kneading inched toward pinching. "Easy, Alec, I have to sit on that later."

He swallowed a laugh. "Sorry. But Giselle sweetie, you do have the most luscious ass." Then his hands moved lower until he was holding her open with his fingers. She could feel herself — everything in her — straining toward him. Silently begging for him.

"Oh, God, Alec..."

"I like that, Giselle. I like hearing you groan my name." He eased into her, inch by delicious inch; she leaned forward and braced her arms on the bed. "Now, if y'don't mind, I'd like to hear you scream it." He thrust, hard.

He stroked, and his hands were everywhere...running up and down her back, cupping her breasts, stroking her nipples...then roughly pulling them between his fingers, as if he instinctively knew when she wanted him to be sweet and when she wanted — needed — him to be rough. She screamed his name, begged him to stop screwing around and *do her, dammit*. He laughed in pure delight, laughed while she writhed and groaned and shoved back at him. Then his strokes pushed her into orgasm and he abruptly quit laughing and gasped instead.

She realized the sun had come up a while ago. Well, who gave a rat's ass? She couldn't believe the man's stamina. She couldn't believe *her* stamina.

"Getting tired?" he panted in her ear. He was still crouched behind her, still filling her the way no man ever had. When he braced himself and thrust, she swore she could feel his cock in her throat. "Giselle? All right?"

"Yes, I'm tired, I'm exhausted, you big dolt, and don't you dare stop."

He chuckled and she could feel his fingers dancing along the length of her spine. Then his hand came around and found her clit. He stroked the throbbing bud with his thumb and said, "I wish my mouth was there right now. Later, it will be," and that was enough, that tipped her into another orgasm.

She felt his grip tighten on her. "Oh, God, that's so sweet," he groaned. "Has anyone told you? When you come, your muscles lock." He shuddered behind her as he at last found his release. "*All* your muscles."

She giggled weakly and rested her head on the bed. Three times...or was that the fourth? The man wasn't human. Thank *God* she was on the Pill.

He stood, then picked her up and cradled her in his arms as if she were a child. "You'll sleep now," he said, laying her in the bed and covering her. "And so will I...you've worn me out, m'lady." Then, incongruously, "Do you have a passport?"

"No," she said drowsily.

"Hmm. I'll have to fix that. Can't come to Scotland without one of those."

"You still want me to come?" She blushed, remember how they'd spent the last five hours. "To Scotland, I mean?"

"Of course." He was arranging the covers over himself, pulling her into his embrace, wrapping his long legs around hers. She was instantly warm and sinfully comfortable. The throbbing between her thighs had finally quit. *It quit because you're numb, you twit. He's fucked you numb. And it was just fine.* "I said, didn't I?"

"Well..." She yawned against his shoulder. "That was before I gave up the goods, so to speak."

"Giselle, darling." He kissed the top of her head. "I've never known a woman so smart and so silly at the same time. You're coming to Scotland. To put it another way, I'm not leaving without you."

"Bossy putz," she muttered. Then squinched her eyes shut as he turned on the bedside light. "Aggh! I think my retinas just fused!"

She could hear him swallow a laugh. "Sorry, love. I just wanted to get a good look at your neck." She felt him push her hair back and gently touch the bite. "A bite's a serious thing...I'm really sorry if I hurt you. You know that, right, Giselle?"

"Don't worry about it. At the risk of making you more arrogant than you already are—though how that's possible I just can't imagine—I loved it. Hardly even hurt."

"Oh." She could hear the unmistakable relief in his tone. "I'm glad t'hear it. I don't have an explanation except…I don't want you to think I go around biting just anybody. I just…lost myself in you."

"That, and you wanted to mark me," she added drowsily. Ah, even with that obnoxious light on, she was going to be able to get to sleep quite nicely. Take that, bedside lamp! "It's all right. I don't mind wearing your mark for a while.

"*What* did you say?"

"Marked me."

"What?"

"Arked-may E-may! Jesus, for a guy with heightened senses you're really slow."

"*What*?"

"Don't yell, I'm right here. I forgot werewolves were so touchy."

"Oh my *God*."

"Steady, pal." Concerned, she sat up. He looked like he was going to pass out. "Hey, it's okay. I said it was, right? You marked me so another werewolf won't take it into his head to jump me. Theoretically, they'll see your mark and steer clear. Or lose their minds and decide, of all things, to fight for me. Ha! Like that'd happen."

She saw him lurch into the chair — sitting down before he fell down. Very wise. "You know? About me?"

"Sure. Not right away," she added comfortingly, since he looked so shattered. "Took me a while to figure it out. But come on, you're a little too quick and too strong for a guy in his — what? Early thirties?"

"Thirty-one," he said absently.

"Plus, your stamina between the sheets was — was really something." Was she blushing? After what they had

just shared? *You're obviously overtired. Go to sleep, Giselle.*
"I've never met one—a werewolf—but my mom used to
work for Lucius Wyndham."

He was staring at her with the most priceless look of
astonishment on his face. "*Your mother worked for the former
pack leader?*"

"Will you *stop* with the yelling? Yes, she managed his
stables for him. 'Course, he couldn't come near any of his
horses without them going crazy trying to get away from
him. He finally had to tell her the truth, because she
thought he'd abused them, and was getting ready to sic
the ASPCA on him.

"Well, of course he wasn't hurting them, it's just
instinctive for horses to stay the hell away from
werewolves. So he told her, and proved it to her, and she
liked the horses, and liked him, and stayed on. 'Til she
married my dad and moved to Boston. But she'd seen a lot
by then. My mom," Giselle added with satisfaction, "tells
the *best* bedtime stories. I figured you out a little while ago.
I said so…remember?"

He was shaking his head, his mouth hanging open. "I
just can't—all night I've been trying to figure out if I
should just kidnap you t'Scotland and tell you the truth
over there—"

"Typical werewolf courtship," she sneered. "You guys
really need to work on the romance thing."

"Or try to explain it to you tomorrow. Later today, I
mean. Or wait until we knew each other better—but you
knew!"

"Yup."

"And you didn't say anything!"

MaryJanice Davidson

"It didn't seem polite, since you didn't bring it up." She blushed harder, like that was possible. "Besides, we...had other things on our minds."

He burst into laughter, great, roaring laughs that made her ears ring. "Giselle sweet, you're for me and I'm *definitely* for you. I knew it the moment I smelled you. Ripe peaches in the middle of all those street smells and slush. The only Santa who was ovulating." He pounced on the bed and pulled her into his arms, kissing her everywhere he could.

"Jeez, cut it out!" She was laughing and trying to fend him off. "Can't we do this later? We ordinary humans get *tired* after making love all night."

"There's nothing ordinary about you, sweetie."

"Oh, come on. You can't tell me that on that whole street, where there were probably a couple hundred people, the only one ovulating was me?"

"No, I can't tell you that." He kissed her on the mouth. "What I can tell you is that the only woman *for me* was ovulating."

"Oh. Sleep now?" she added helpful, groping for the bedside lamp.

He shut the light off for her. "Scotland?"

"Yes."

"Forever?"

"Nope. Sorry, my parents are from here. I have friends here, too. A life I made before I ever laid eyes on you, pretty boy. And, hello? Courtship, anybody? It'd be nice to date a little, before we got married."

He mock-sighed. "Humans, oh, Lord help me. A house in Boston, then, but at least half the year at my

186

family home. After," he sighed again, "an appropriately lengthy courtship."

"Done."

"Naked courtship?" he asked hopefully.

She laughed. "We'll work out the details. Doesn't really matter, though. Wither thou goest, I will go. And all that."

"And all that," he said, and kissed her smiling mouth.

About the authors:

Lani Aames, Treva Harte, and MaryJanice Davidson welcome mail from readers. You can write to them c/o Ellora's Cave Publishing at P.O. Box 787, Hudson, Ohio 44236-0787.

Also by Lani Aames:

- Desperate Hearts
- Lusty Charms: Invictus
- Things That Go Bump In the Night II – anthology with MaryJanice Davidson & Margaret Carter

Also by Treva Harte:

- Intimate Choices
- His Mistress
- The Seduction of Sean Nolan
- Wicked
- Why Me?
- The Deviants
- Changing the Odds
- World Enough
- The Wildling
- Perfect
- No Time To Dream
- Things That Go Bump In the Night – anthology with Jaid Black & Marilyn Lee
- Twisted Destiny – anthology with Sherri King & S.L. Carpenter
- Threshold – anthology with Kate Douglas

Also by MaryJanice Davidson:

- Thief of Hearts
- Canis Royal: Bridefight
- Love Lies
- Things That Go Bump In the Night II – anthology with MaryJanice Davidson & Margaret Carter

Why an electronic book?

We live in the Information Age—an exciting time in the history of human civilization in which technology rules supreme and continues to progress in leaps and bounds every minute of every hour of every day. For a multitude of reasons, more and more avid literary fans are opting to purchase e-books instead of paperbacks. The question to those not yet initiated to the world of electronic reading is simply: *why?*

Price. An electronic title at Ellora's Cave Publishing runs anywhere from 40-75% less than the cover price of the <u>exact same title</u> in paperback format. Why? Cold mathematics. It is less expensive to publish an e-book than it is to publish a paperback, so the savings are passed along to the consumer.

Space. Running out of room to house your paperback books? That is one worry you will never have with electronic novels. For a low one-time cost, you can purchase a handheld computer designed specifically for e-reading purposes. Many e-readers are larger than the average handheld, giving you plenty of screen room. Better yet, hundreds of titles can be stored within your new library—a single microchip. (Please note that Ellora's Cave does not endorse any specific brands. You can check our website at www.ellorascave.com for customer recommendations we make available to new consumers.)

Mobility. Because your new library now consists of only a microchip, your entire cache of books can be taken with you wherever you go.

Personal preferences are accounted for. Are the words you are currently reading too small? Too **large**? Too...**ANNOYING**? Paperback books cannot be modified according to personal preferences, but e-books can.

Innovation. The *way* you read a book is not the only advancement the Information Age has gifted the literary community with. There is also the factor of what you can read. Ellora's Cave Publishing will be introducing a new line of interactive titles that are available in e-book format only.

Instant gratification. Is it the middle of the night and all the bookstores are closed? Are you tired of waiting days — sometimes weeks — for online and offline bookstores to ship the novels you bought? Ellora's Cave Publishing sells instantaneous downloads 24 hours a day, 7 days a week, 365 days a year. Our e-book delivery system is 100% automated, meaning your order is filled as soon as you pay for it.

Those are a few of the top reasons why electronic novels are displacing paperbacks for many an avid reader. As always, Ellora's Cave Publishing welcomes your questions and comments. We invite you to email us at service@ellorascave.com or write to us directly at: P.O. Box 787, Hudson, Ohio 44236-0787.

Printed in the United States
1456900001B/67